Witch and Famous

~ Presented by J.R. Rain Press ~

WITCH AND FAMOUS

(The Witch Detectives #2)

by

Eve Paludan and Stuart Sharp

BOOKS BY EVE PALUDAN

SERIES

WITCH DETECTIVES (Eve Paludan and Stuart Sharp)
Witchy Business
Witch and Famous
Witch Way Out (coming soon)

ANGEL DETECTIVES
The Man Who Fell from the Sky

WEREWOLF DETECTIVES
Werewolf Interrupted (coming soon)

J.R. Rain's
BROTHERHOOD OF THE BLADE TRILOGY
by Eve Paludan
Burning
Afterglow
Radiance (coming soon)

Scott Nicholson and J.R. Rain's
GHOST FILES
Ghost Fire

RANCH LOVERS ROMANCE
Taking Back Tara
Tara Takes Christmas

SINGLE TITLES

Letters from David
Finding Jessie
Chasing Broadway

BOOKS BY STUART SHARP

Court of Dreams

The characters and events portrayed in this book are fictitious. Any similarity to real persons, living or dead, is coincidental and not intended by the author.

Printed in the United States of America.

Published by Eve Paludan

ISBN-13: 978-1490935942
ISBN-10: 1490935940

Cover design: David H. Doucot
Editor: Tracy Seybold

Acknowledgments

My heartfelt thanks go to J.R. Rain for your energetic inspiration, encouragement and enthusiasm.

Stuart Sharp, thank you for your hard work on The Witch Detectives series. I had so much fun with this collaboration. It is my honor and privilege to work with an author of your talent, caliber, credentials, and work ethic. — *Eve Paludan*

Contents

* Chapter One *

"We all have our secrets."
— Samantha Moon in *Vampire Dawn*

I shouldn't have eaten that eel pie and mash last night. The fallout of my midnight snack with Niall was that I dreamed I was a mermaid—and my silvery tail was tangled in a fishing net.

I screamed underwater, but Niall couldn't hear me. My words soundlessly bubbled up to the bright surface, where I could see Niall sitting on the dock, dangling his legs over the water. Below me, the darkness of the deep held the secrets I needed to escape, but I was afraid to see exactly what they were.

As I struggled to free my tail from the net, something pulled me toward the bottom of a loch where Nessie lurked, waiting for me to come closer…

Just as I saw amber sea serpent eyes open, two things woke me up from that vivid nightmare. First, there was my phone, with a text from Siobhan telling me to meet her at the Fringe for new information. More than that though, there was the hunger that gnawed at me like fangs gnashing against my psyche. It was the hunger I'd learned to live with over the past few weeks, since I'd learned the truth about what I was.

The enchantress in me was clearly hungry.

I blinked against the sunlight that dappled Niall's master bedroom and unwound my legs from his tempest-tossed linens. Those were wrapped, cocoon-like, around my bare legs. Presumably, it had been those dragging me down into the depths in my dream. I didn't want to think about what else it might have been.

Being Niall's lover was sublime. I sighed in contentment as the previous night came back to me in a rush. However, after a memorable night that ranged from tender emotional connection to sizzling passion that defied words and escaped only through cries, Niall seemed to have fled from his house before I woke. Again. All I could think of was that he must really dread those awkward morning-after moments—he always disappeared without waking me.

Always. He'd been gone when I awoke every morning since we started sleeping together. At first, I thought it was just the need to take things slowly, the restlessness of being in bed with someone new. Now, weeks into our relationship, I knew better. Niall and I slept together, but waking up together seemed to be a different question entirely.

Shaking off the nightmare, I dressed and headed downstairs. I checked in the living room, where there was still no sign of Niall, and checked my phone, in case this was the time that he had left me an explanation. Nothing. At least not from him. Instead, I found a text waiting for me from my goblin contact, Siobhan.

Meet me at the Fringe. Bring cash. I have information.

Siobhan was a goblin and a thief, but she was also one of my better sources of information on everything that went on in Edinburgh's underworlds. Both the criminal one and the more literal one occupied by the goblins.

I headed out of the back of Niall's town house through the open garage doors. I decided to take a shortcut to the festival to meet Siobhan and perhaps use the Fringe's sea of emotions to put off the less physical hunger that I felt a little longer. I couldn't feed from a crowd—emotions I tried to take snapped back to their owners without a break in the body's defenses—but I could at least ride the highs and lows of the crowd's feelings. I could always get some more human breakfast from the food stalls.

As I headed through the garage, David, Niall's driver, was polishing the chrome trim on the sleek black Lexus that served as Niall's car when showing up in the Aston Martin wasn't quite right for the occasion. He looked up as I passed.

"Wait, Miss Chambers. Please? Mr. Sampson asked me to give you a ride this morning to wherever you wanted to go."

"Hi, David. I don't really need a ride, thanks." I swallowed as I realized this was probably the best chance I was going to get all morning to feed. "But I do sort of need… sustenance."

I sighed, embarrassed.

"I understand," he said. "Luckily for both of us, I nicked myself shaving this morning. It should make things easier." He bent down to my height, his skin just inches from my face.

I gulped. Since they were among the few humans who knew what we were, Niall's staff were a lot more understanding about my feeding needs than anyone else would have been. I'd been feeding from them since Niall had showed me what I was. An enchantress. An emotional vampire, able to take feelings and manipulate them, the way

I'd always been told I could, but also able to use them as fuel for magic. I needed them to survive, now that I had embraced my power.

That was the hard part.

I took a deep, shuddering breath and pressed my lips tightly against David's clean-shaven neck at the site of a small nick in the skin—skin that smelled of fragrant vetiver aftershave. The placement of the cut was unfortunate. It reminded me too much of all the classic images of vampires, when a pinprick to the finger would have done the job just as well.

Or a kiss, but there was only one person I kissed, and that was Niall.

I fed—possibly a little too greedily. I sucked down emotion and energy through that tiny break in the skin. I could taste the blood there, but that had nothing to do with it. People always made too much of the blood. It was just a way in. If it were just about the blood, I could get some from a hospital or a slaughterhouse, rather than having to feed on living, breathing humans with real emotions.

Speaking of which, David's feelings were absolutely *delicious*. What a glorious way to wake up in the morning. After a minute or so, he swayed a bit and I took that as my signal to pull back. It wasn't easy.

"Are you all right?" I asked. My pulse sang in my veins as I said it.

He nodded. "Fine. Just fine."

He didn't look fine. He was far too pale, for one thing. David sat down heavily on a small stool in the car garage.

"You're sure you are fine?"

"Perfectly fine, Ms. Chambers."

"Look, I'm going to walk this morning. Should I call Marie for you, or help you to your quarters to rest, maybe?"

"No." He sounded a little startled at the offer to help him back to his room. Maybe he thought there was more to the offer than I intended. "No, I'm just going to sit here for a minute. I'm sure everything is fine, Ms. Chambers."

"It's really about time you called me Elle," I said. "Is it like this when Niall takes energy from you?"

"Mr. Sampson makes his own arrangements."

Meaning that he didn't feed from his driver. Well, *that* didn't exactly make me feel better. I squeezed David's shoulder reassuringly, but couldn't help grabbing a couple more morsels of emotion through the cut while I did it. I glanced away in shame, stepping back from him. He was a human being, not a breakfast snack.

Although he had done the same job. Briefly, and I knew it would only be briefly, the hunger faded into the background. David nodded politely and I went on my way, my energy high for once. To take my mind off what I'd just done, I wondered what information Siobhan had to sell to me today. Something to do with a stolen item I could locate for an insurer, maybe? I hoped so. I needed all the cases I could get.

I headed off to meet her.

Chapter Two

Edinburgh's Fringe Festival brought out the best and the worst in performers. You could see more entertainment here than almost anywhere else during festival month, but that competition also made performers pretty desperate to impress. More than once already this month, I'd had to use my talents simply to persuade would-be comedians that no, I really *didn't* want a flier.

Even this early in the morning, the streets were alive. That was one thing about living in Edinburgh: you either learned to embrace the festival excitement, or you effectively moved out of the city for the month. I loved the shows and the food, but I'd always been stuck firmly in the latter camp.

Until recently, I hadn't had the choice. With that much emotion about…well, August was the month I usually left on holiday. This year though…well, this year, I had Niall; he'd said he was bound by the demands of his business deals to stay in the city.

In reality, I think he was trying to force me to stay and see it all. Showing me again that I wouldn't be overwhelmed by the emotion the way I'd always been taught. Until I met him, I'd worked so hard to push away emotional hotspots. I hadn't even been able to set foot in a nightclub. Every year, I'd gone somewhere else. Now, I had *this.*

I watched a quartet of Great Highland bagpipers and drummers for a while, soaking in their passion for their music as they belted out reinterpretations of the top forty. This was the Fringe, after all, rather than the festival proper. Enjoying the reactions of the crowd around me, it must have been about the first time I'd ever *enjoyed* bagpipes. It was a windy day and they were all wearing kilts, so there was some fun to be had there, too.

My phone went off. Frankly, over the bagpipes, I barely heard it. There was a reason the Scots used to take them into war with them. I looked at the caller ID and walked off so I could return my phone call without being deafened.

"Hello, Elle. Thanks for returning my call so quickly."

"What's up, Fergie?"

Fergie was my legal assistant—a lawyer who had moved to the city to be nearer his elderly mother. He was also a werewolf.

"Have you, by any chance, seen Siobhan today?" Fergie asked.

"As a matter of fact, we're meeting this morning. I haven't seen her yet. You know how goblins are good at sticking to the shadows. I'm sure she'll show up soon, though. She texted me that she has some new information for me."

"Really? And of course she wants payment for that information?"

"Yes." She *was* an informant by profession. Well, when she wasn't being a thief. "What is it about Siobhan this morning?"

Fergie hesitated a moment. "I'm worried about her…"

"Is this the 'she's a thief and you can't trust her' conversation again?" I asked. Apparently, my werewolf lawyer had this thing about known thieves. "Because we've been through this, Fergie. I know Siobhan. I *like* Siobhan."

"It's a little more specific," Fergie said. "This morning, when I unlocked the office, no one was here, but I detected the after-scent of goblins in the conference room, specifically, on the couch, the conference table, and the carpet."

I grimaced. "Goblins, as in plural?"

"Yes. Male and female."

"Oh, wonderful," I said, my heart sinking. I only knew one goblin couple, in the form of Siobhan and her boyfriend, Dougie. I didn't like Dougie. I *really* didn't like the thought of him and Siobhan having sex on my conference table. Get a room. One that didn't belong to me. "Is anything missing from the office?"

"The computers are all here, but they have been moved a bit. You know how I like things to be orderly."

That was putting it mildly. When I'd hired him, I hadn't known that years of obsessing about a combination of the phases of the moon and the minor details of tort law had left Fergie more than a little OCD about these things.

"Siobhan and her friend have left some things askew. Crumbs are about. Pens and papers, receipt books and legal forms—small things of that sort—have been moved in our supply closet, as if someone was looking for something. So far, we do have one casualty."

"Oh no. What's gone missing?" I asked.

"My mum's leftover haggis, neeps and tatties from the office refrigerator. I'm guessing it was their breakfast."

"Neeps and tatties?" I smiled. "You realize that you're a walking stereotype, Ferguson Black? Why not just have everything deep fried and have done with it?"

"I *like* neeps."

I smiled at that. "Take some money out of petty cash for your lunch today. I'll talk to Siobhan about unwanted sleepovers. Is that everything that's missing?"

"I'll check. Give me a minute." I heard him rustling around in the background. After a few moments, he said, "Elle, we have a bigger problem than I thought. The petty cash box has been snatched. It was in a locked file cabinet."

I groaned. Even for Siobhan, there were lines. "I'll deal with this, Fergie."

"Um, you aren't going to do anything…"

"I'm not going to do anything illegal. Or dangerous. You think I'd drain someone over this? I'm not a monster, Fergie."

"I never said you were." He sighed. "Look, I don't want to get Siobhan in trouble or make her lose her occasional jobs with you. I just don't want her compromising the security at the office, and she has done *exactly* that. She's sneaking in and sleeping there, stealing from us."

"They probably don't have another place to sleep and they're broke," I pointed out. "We can replace the food and cash."

The trust would be harder.

Fergie paused. He knew that it was my call to make. I was the boss. "So, what should we do about it? I called you first, rather than ring the police."

"You did the right thing," I assured him. The last thing we needed was the police trying to investigate purely supernatural affairs. "Change the door alarm code. I'll deal with the rest."

"What do you want me to change it to?"

"I'll text you the number after we hang up."

"All right."

"And, Fergie? Could you sniff around so that we're certain about how she got in? If she's squeezing through the attic or coming in through a window with her delinquent boyfriend... well, that leaves our office wide open for a huge goblin invasion." I thought about some of my other employers. "It also doesn't do our insurance premiums much good."

"I'll track her scent to figure out how she got in here."

"Thanks."

"No problem. Don't let her get away with this, though."

"Fergie." I didn't let my tone sharpen, but he had to know what I meant. He'd had his say. I would deal with this. "Siobhan's good at what she does."

"That's true. If you want to recover stolen property, get a goblin thief as an informant."

I laughed.

"Oh, I do have other news," Fergie said in a different tone.

"What is it?" I asked. I was probably about to get a rundown of the minor details of a couple of insurance claims. For a fearsome shape-shifting creature out of myth, it turned out that Fergie was mostly very good at paperwork.

"Three things, actually. I have been working on background investigations on the coven. You know that they're still talking about the possibility of getting rid of you?"

"How did you find that out?"

"I have a contact who infiltrated the coven."

"What? Who?"

He paused. "Me."

"You?" I asked, surprised. I stepped further away from the crowds, into a spot of shade off the street.

"It's amazing what people will say when a friendly lawyer pops round to discuss their legal position regarding you.

Especially when they don't know that lawyer can hear like me and start talking outside the room. I also did some digging into the paperwork around them. Their companies, deals, minutes and so on. During the course of that, I've found out a few things. I think I should probably discuss a couple of them with you in person."

"You can tell me that the coven might want to kill me over the phone, but not this part?"

"The coven already know that you know they want you gone," Fergie pointed out. "This part… it's more important that I tell you face to face."

"Intriguing," I said. "Wait, you said three pieces of news. What's the third piece of news?"

"The *Bewitched* DVD that you ordered to replace the one that wore out has arrived." There was undisguised mirth in his voice.

That was good enough news that I forgot to tell him how stupid just walking up to the coven and listening in on it was. "Fergie, you just made my day."

He laughed heartily. "Why do you like that TV show so much?"

"Are you kidding?" I said. "A witch who has to keep her magic a secret from mortals? I'll bring you some haggis from the festival to replace your stolen lunch."

"Perfect."

I shook my head. Some people would eat anything.

We hung up and I immediately texted Fergie my new code for the office door. *1873.* The year Niall was born. Also, the code I'd used to shut down the alarms in his gallery, immediately before proving that he'd stolen one of his own paintings just to meet me. It would be very easy for me to remember.

I looked around some more for Siobhan. Further along, there was a magician, doing street magic, making objects appear and disappear. Funny that people could get so much enjoyment from a little sleight of hand, when they would probably have run screaming from *real* magic.

I still didn't see Siobhan, but I did feel her. There was a tang to goblin emotions that was as distinctive as the taste of the haggis Fergie wanted. Though possibly slightly more palatable. Siobhan was nearby, but so were hundreds of other people. *Where was she?* She'd been late before, but with the information that Fergie had given me, would she even show up? Would she have second thoughts?

I stretched out my senses, searching for her as I bought haggis, potatoes and turnips for Fergie. I carefully placed the take-away container in the bottom of my tote bag. I was finding out that werewolves had almost insatiable appetites. Had Fergie been completely human, he would have been just another part of Scotland's dire national obesity statistics. Fortunately, as a werewolf, he burned off the calories at an astounding rate.

I walked further down the street, trying to hone in on Siobhan. It wasn't easy because her energy was moving around quickly, darting in and out of the throng. I stopped at a spot where the crowd was exclaiming over a fire-eater's act. I stopped to watch it and basked in the energy of the crowd, captivated by the illusion of danger. As someone who had been on the receiving end of real blasts of power, a few flares of flame were nicely relaxing by comparison. It was a strange kind of double pleasure. I was getting the thrill of the performance for myself, and then the reaction of the crowd a fraction of a second later.

It was strange to think that until recently, so much emotion in one place had been enough to make me close myself off, shut myself down, and generally give myself a headache trying to keep it all out. It was, as I had been taught in childhood, just one of the many downsides of being an enchantress who was able to use magic to affect others' emotions. They—by which I mean the coven, my mother, and every tutor I'd had—had taught me that something like this would kill me or send me mad, cripple me with sensory overload or destroy my mind trying to make sense of it. They'd lied to me. Perhaps some of them, like my mother, had done it to protect me, but far more had been scared.

To everyone around me, I probably looked no different to anyone else. A little prettier than most of the people there, maybe. A little more attractive in some way that they couldn't quite put their finger on, thanks to the backwash of my power, but otherwise, I was just your average thirty-five-year-old Scottish woman in casual clothes with flame-colored hair and high-cheekbones.

Yet, the truth was that I was an emotional vampire, capable of sucking the living energy right out of someone. I was capable of using that power to work effects that more than made up for the years when I thought I hadn't been able to cast even the simplest of witch spells as my mother had.

Possibly the best part, though, was that it meant I could walk through the middle of a crowd like this with my shields down, letting the emotions run through me as a would-be comedian juggled knives to try to get the crowd's attention, the expectation there from the crowd, the concentration from the performer…

A sudden flash of anger cut through all of it. I whirled around just a moment before I heard someone yell, "Stop, thieves!"

✱ Chapter Three ✱

I felt them before I saw them, but I saw them quickly enough, too. Two hooded figures sprinted away through the crowd at a speed that should have sent people around them sprawling but didn't. The ease with which they dodged through the crowd told me they had done this before. Maybe if one of them hadn't happened to glance back right then, I would have just left it alone. I was an insurance investigator, after all, not the police. The trouble was, I recognized the pale, scale-marred features that stared back at me. Features I'd been searching for almost since I stepped outside this morning.

"Siobhan!" I yelled. It was a wonder that about five women didn't turn toward me. After all, it wasn't exactly an uncommon name in Scotland, and Edinburgh was a large city. As it was though, only one reacted, and she did it by running faster.

I took off after *my* Siobhan and her accomplice, pulling in emotion from the crowd to fuel my body's hot pursuit, even as I reached out mentally to encourage people not to interfere. The last thing I wanted anyone doing was trying to grab a goblin. Goblins varied a lot, but the one thing it was easy to say with certainty was that any human trying to grab one would get a nasty surprise. Especially if they tried to grab Dougie. I knew from experience that he liked blades. Even Siobhan...

Well, it was simple. The term "goblin" was slang for any fey dangerous to humans. An old word that had somehow come to mean something far more specific, probably thanks to Tolkien. People thought they were all small, green, and stupid. None of that necessarily applied. The dangerous to humans part still did though, which was why I needed to keep them away. I didn't count. I had *never* counted as just human, even before I found out the full depth of what I was. If I couldn't handle a pair of goblin teens, I'd better just go back to my mother's books and study.

My feet pounded the pavement as I ran, using the crowd's energy to power my sprint after the goblins, dodging around people where I had to, but mostly just making them step aside before it became necessary.

"Siobhan, Dougie, *stop*!" I put power into that word, using the energy of the crowd around me to turn it into a command. I couldn't take over their minds and make them do what I wanted, but I could throw a suggestion at them with enough force to make them hesitate. A second or two of hesitation was all I needed to catch up to them.

They whirled toward me, the alarm on their faces obvious at my presence. Apparently, even though they had been planning to meet me, they hadn't expected me to show up when they were in the middle of stealing from someone.

Siobhan was actually quite pretty by goblin standards. It was simply that goblin standards were so alien that most of the time, they came across as weird and otherworldly. If she'd been human, I would have put her in her late teens. The hair sticking out from under the hood was a blonde so pale that it was close to white, while her features had patches of silvery scales like a fish's skin. Or a lizard's.

Dougie was mostly just a bundle of sullenness in a hooded top. After centuries of banishment from the daylight world, goblins didn't like the sun much. He glared openly at me, and the animosity was clearly mutual.

I sensed mostly fear and anxiety from Siobhan. For all that they could be dangerous, goblins weren't known for their magic. They couldn't shut me out like a powerful witch could. Even for a goblin, Siobhan had almost no shields. Dougie was only a little harder to read. Judging by the way Siobhan was looking at him, he obviously had a certain icky romantic appeal, at least by goblin standards. The best that I could say was that he did have better teeth than most goblins.

"I said stop!" I repeated, when Dougie grabbed Siobhan's hand to run away again. He froze and she bumped into him. She deserved more than this opportunistic loser.

Dougie half-snarled at me, and I held out my hand with a sigh.

"Hand it over, Dougie. Whatever you took, give it up. The last time we played this game, I knocked you down and nearly broke your arm. That was before I even knew what I was. Now…I am sure that Siobhan has informed you what I could do to you."

He stuck out his chin in a defiant way that said he knew all about me, but he wasn't scared. It would have worked better if I couldn't feel the fear underneath thrumming away like the dull beat of a drum. Of course, even a frightened thug could be dangerous, when cornered.

"Are you really sure you want to play this game now?" I asked. "With me?"

He looked like he might be prepared to try it anyway, but Siobhan put a hand on his arm.

"Give her the cell phone, Dougie," she said. "Elle isn't going to hand us over to the police. Or the coven."

I wasn't sure I liked the certainty there, but she *was* right about that. I didn't want the police finding out about goblins any more than the rest of humanity. The last thing we needed was for them to know about the creatures living among them. In this case, in tunnels running through the dead volcano under Edinburgh.

As for the coven…well, I had a few problems with an institution whose approach to the non-human was to kill it the moment it became a problem. I had already had one close call when it came to my former coven contact, Rebecca, and a warlock whom Niall and I had overcome together when he'd tried an assassination attempt.

That didn't mean I was letting Dougie and Siobhan get away with stealing, though.

"The phone," I said quietly, but with a firmness designed to let Dougie know I meant business. Dougie handed Siobhan a new-looking Android phone. Siobhan was the one who handed it to me. Maybe Dougie didn't want me touching him. People could sometimes be picky about that kind of thing once they knew what I was. They thought a touch would be enough to drain them. They weren't quite right, but I wasn't going to tell Dougie that.

"I thought I told you to leave this idiot?" I said to her quietly.

She gave me one of those complex shrugs that only teenagers seem to be able to manage. "You aren't my mother."

Now there was a whole argument I didn't want to have.

"Dougie, where's what you took from my office?" I asked, narrowing my eyes at him.

Siobhan looked shocked. "Did you steal something from Elle's office last night?"

"I don't have your petty cash box," he said, with what he probably intended to be defiance.

I'd had enough. "Dougie, you know I can *feel* when you're scared, right?" I took half a step toward him. "Not to mention the part where I never said anything about a petty cash box. Where's the money that was in it?"

"Spent," he admitted, after a sullen second or two of standing there, obviously trying to work out if he could get away with any other answer.

Siobhan stared at him in obvious shock. It was nice to know that she hadn't known about that part. "On what?"

"Stuff." Dougie shrugged. "None of your business."

Siobhan looked like she might cry. That or hit him. I wasn't sure which, even with my powers.

Back to the issue at hand.

"Siobhan, who does this cell phone belong to?" I asked.

"He's coming." She angled her head at someone coming through the crowd with a purposeful stride. I could feel the anger coming off him at having been stolen from. Siobhan was probably just good at keeping an eye on marks.

Since I couldn't afford the approaching man going to the police, I held up the phone and nodded at him. I added the nicest smile I had. Not to mention just a trace of power. From the way he checked me out as he approached, I knew it had worked.

"Is this yours?" I asked.

"I think that's mine, yes," he said a little breathlessly. He turned it on, checking it. "You caught the thieves involved?"

"No thieves." I treated him to another smile. "There seems to have been a terrible misunderstanding. These youths thought it was their phone." I pushed a little harder. I needed him to trust me. This was one side of my powers I'd used plenty of times. Even the coven had used me for this. Smoothing over…incidents. "They picked it up by mistake."

"Oh, thank goodness I have it back. I'm traveling on business and I would be lost without my phone!" he said. "I couldn't believe it when they picked it up off the table while I was eating."

I handed it to him. "You know how alike phone cases look." It wasn't an explanation, not really. Without the steady stream of power I was pushing into him, he would never have believed it. Never have *trusted* me enough to believe it. I wasn't hypnotizing him, exactly. I couldn't put thoughts in his head, but I *could* influence what he felt so much that he would believe almost anything I said.

"I don't think the boy realized his girlfriend had theirs in her pocket. Sorry."

"These things happen," the man said. "Nice of you to straighten things out. Um…you wouldn't be interested in getting a drink sometime, would you?"

"I'm with someone," I said.

"Even so…"

Maybe I'd overdone things. Certainly, it took another flicker of magic before he turned away, going to take a call.

Of course, by that point, Siobhan and Dougie had gone.

Thieves! Not just thieves but *goblin* thieves! Goblin thieves, in Siobhan's case, who didn't listen to me. Was there *no* way to get Siobhan to dump Dougie for her own good? Maybe a strong dose of my power? Goblins had not much more of a wall around their emotions than humans, so I might be able to achieve something if I tried.

Only that would be wrong. I was *not* going to use my power to push them to break up. I didn't have the right, even when I thought it would be for the best. Siobhan needed to make that decision for herself. It was still a mystery to me why she would ever want to be with Dougie, though. Either it was blind infatuation or Siobhan had a very compelling reason not to walk away from an idiot like him.

It occurred to me that I wasn't going to be getting information from Siobhan today. That was a pity. She was a good source of information down in goblin territory, not to mention anything on the less legal side of life in the capital. It was just that Dougie was such a bad influence on her behavior above ground. As for below ground… who knew what goblins did there? I'd certainly never been near their home. Outsiders kept out or they didn't come back.

I sighed and made my way toward my offices, where I'd been planning to go once I'd gotten what I needed from Siobhan. At least, before I started playing chase with a couple of tear-away goblins. Couldn't *one* day in my job be straightforward?

* Chapter Four *

The office was new. It was my concession to the fact that, if I was going to make a living now that the coven hated me, I needed to expand my business beyond just the gigs that I got through them and a couple of trusted insurers. That meant prestige. Stability. Enough room to actually accommodate my legal advisor.

I'd acquired office space above a firm of accountants, some cheap office furniture, even a simple website proclaiming me open for business. Fergie had built the website. Combine that with his spying on the coven, and I was starting to believe he had many untapped talents.

"Hi, Elle." Fergie was waiting for me when I got in, looking very smart in a neatly tailored, if slightly worn, suit. Although his dark hair did stick up at rakish, untamable angles, he didn't make my heart rate increase like Niall did. Possibly, it was just something about the word 'lawyer.' Or possibly not. "I didn't know when you'd be back to the office."

"Text me anytime," I said. "Here's your haggis, tatties and neeps." I handed him the take-away container. "I still don't know how you can eat them."

"These are wonderful. Thank you." Fergie smiled at me in such an open way that I couldn't help smiling back.

"Want to eat lunch with me today?" I asked. When he held up the box, I shook my head. "I'll be having salad."

Fergie started to smile, but then stopped himself. "I think you might already have plans. Niall's in your inner office waiting for you."

"Niall's here?" Here when he hadn't been back at his own house. His comings and goings were proving increasingly impossible to keep track of.

Fergie nodded. "Another time then?"

"Sure. Why not?"

I only hoped Fergie wasn't looking for anything out of lunch with me beyond the meal. Oh, Fergie was pretty good looking, in an outdoorsy kind of way, yet next to the impeccable man who sat on the edge of my desk, there was no comparison.

I walked into my inner sanctum and smiled a hello. "Niall. What a lovely surprise! What are you doing here?"

He did come down to my work place, but not that often. He had plenty of his own, after all, even if I'd never been entirely clear on what he did. There was a little talk about deals from his PA, Marie, but beyond that, I'd never asked for the details.

"Hello, Elle. Have a bit of excitement down at the Fringe Festival?" Niall asked, cocking his head.

"How…" I paused. I knew how he could do it. The same way I would. He could feel the mix of emotions that still clung to me in the aftermath of my encounter with the goblins. It didn't mean he knew details, just that something had happened. "It was… interesting."

"Tell me."

"In a bit," I said. I would much rather look at him than talk about Dougie. Niall was, quite simply, the best-looking man I'd ever seen, and I didn't just think that was just because he happened to be the man I loved. Or just because he had the preternatural attractiveness of any enchanter/vampire. Dressed in a full three-piece suit that would have made anyone else look like they were in a costume for the festival, he simply looked perfect, like a Renaissance artist's model who had stopped off in a nineteenth-century tailor on his way to the present.

"Niall?" I kissed him. I couldn't be in the same room as him and not kiss him. I'd discovered that at some length over the past few weeks. I'd also discovered that he very rarely opened any conversation by just coming out with what he wanted. "What are you *really* doing here?"

"I really came to take you to lunch," Niall answered, his arms still around me. He looked me up and down. "You still haven't told me about the festival. Did something…strange happen?"

"It wasn't anything important." I knew he was still worried about the idea that the coven might come after us. My former friend, Rebecca, had supposedly fixed it so that they wouldn't, but since she had already tried to kill me once, we couldn't take that as a given.

"What happened at the Fringe?" Niall asked again.

"I just had to stop a couple of goblins from stealing some tourist's phone."

"You *had* to do it?" Niall looked over at Fergie through the open door. "Mr. Black, is there any law in this country that requires someone to hunt down thieves?"

Fergie shrugged. "Well, there used to be the old hue and cry laws, but those haven't been in force for—"

"We get the idea, Fergie." I shook my head in exasperation. "Niall, I'm in a job that involves helping people."

"For money, in certain specified circumstances. You investigate insurance claims. That isn't the same as getting into all-out brawls with goblins."

"It wasn't an all-out brawl," I insisted. "Besides, Siobhan was there. I wanted to keep her out of trouble. Especially when keeping her out of trouble means that we give the coven fewer reasons to come to Edinburgh. If goblins are causing trouble, what do you *think* they'll do?"

Niall had to acknowledge that point, surely? Even so, he still seemed put out that I'd been involved in something like this. I knew that most of it was probably just his concern for my safety, but I was fine. I could have taken on half a dozen goblins. *Probably.*

"How much power did you have to use to catch them?" Niall asked.

"Not much." I shrugged. "It all came out of the crowd, anyway."

Niall shook his head, stepping back from me. "No, Elle. I have told you, it doesn't work like that. Crowds are good for magic and for boosting your body, but you still burn your reserves. I know you still aren't feeding. Not the right way."

Ah, so that was why he was here. He wanted to have *this* conversation. Well, if he thought I was just going to give in on this, he needed to think again.

"I know I skipped Marie yesterday, but she was looking too tired," I offered, by way of an explanation. A way not to fight, at least.

"Which is why I have said all along that your current ways of feeding can be no more than temporary," Niall shot back.

My current ways of feeding. They involved either taking energy secondhand from Niall as he chose to give it to me, or taking energy through small, pinprick wounds on people we knew who didn't mind, like Niall's employees. Neither method was the way that Niall thought I ought to feed. He'd been very clear on that.

"So, when you came here to offer to 'take me to lunch'…" I prompted.

"I meant that I would take you to lunch. Food that is cooked and prepared." Niall looked affronted. "I have reservations."

"Not as many as I think I have right now." I gave him a stern look. He looked back inscrutably. "You really aren't about to push some unsuspecting human my way?"

"I simply intended lunch. However, if on the way, you should happen to find a suitable energy donor, would that be such a bad thing?"

"Is it a bad thing?" I echoed. "Just grabbing some random man or woman, using my powers to seduce them, and then stealing their energy with a kiss? You don't see anything wrong with that? Even when you are the one in an intimate relationship with me?"

Niall frowned. Of course, he frowned. He seemed to be frowning a lot these days. "It is how I have fed for almost my whole life. It is the safest way to feed, Elle. No one realizes what we are doing. We can stay safe. We can stay secret."

Because secrets were so important to him. I didn't say what I was thinking. When we had met, he'd kept the secret of what he was from me, preferring to manipulate me in a game of his own devising. The truth was, Niall liked keeping secrets. There was so much I didn't know about him that I still almost feared to find out. I still didn't even know, for example, where he'd been born, how he'd come into his powers, or how he'd made most of his considerable wealth.

"So, you'd be okay with me just going out and kissing some other guy?" I asked again. I wanted to be clear about it. In the background, the office phone rang. I ignored it. Let Fergie take it. I heard him answer it and speak in soft tones. I tried to follow what Fergie was saying but now, Niall was talking, too.

"It is what we are, Elle," Niall said. "It is what we do."

I shook my head. "It isn't what *I* do."

"Only because you are too stubborn."

"Excuse me," Fergie said, interrupting as he came back into my inner office.

"Not now, please, Fergie."

He looked affronted. How about if I kissed Fergie in front of Niall? Maybe Niall would understand what I was saying *then*. Of course, the only problem with that was that I didn't *want* to kiss Fergie. He was handsome, he was sweet and honest. He was also a werewolf. Nor did I want to kiss anyone else, for that matter. That was kind of the point. So, it would hardly be winning the argument to do that in the hopes of making Niall jealous.

Fergie cleared his throat politely. "Elle?"

"Just a *moment*, Fergie." I'd told him once. I looked at Niall again. "*I'm* stubborn?"

"You think that you can rearrange the world to suit your sensibilities," Niall said. "That things will change if only you refuse to acknowledge them long enough. Yet, ultimately, it causes more pain."

"How so?"

"Did you know that David fainted as he got into the car to drive me over?"

"No. Is he all right?" It was hard to argue when Niall dropped news like that in my lap. Yet, I had to keep going, didn't I? This was why Niall had come round. Another secret. Another attempt to manipulate me.

Niall nodded. "He will be, this time."

"Excuse me, Elle," Fergie said again, "I know this isn't a great time but—"

"Then I just need to take less, don't I?" I said to Niall, ignoring Fergie and trying not to think about what might have happened if David had fainted a little later, while the vehicle was in motion. The thought of the driver being hurt was bad enough. The thought that Niall might have been hurt as well was almost painful.

"No," Niall insisted, "you need to take *more*. You ration yourself too much as it is, but this oh-so-sanitary feeding policy of yours…"

I waited, wanting to hear him say it at last. We needed to have this argument. We'd *been* having this argument off and on almost since we defeated Rebecca and Evert, the warlock hunter whom the coven had sent for us—the hunter we'd killed. Day to day, things were great with Niall. In bed, they were amazing, but this issue was always there in the background, pricking at us. Yes, let Niall finally say what he thought.

"This can't wait, Elle," Fergie finally said. "I'm sorry but it is a matter of—"

"Fergie, what *is* it?" I asked, since we weren't going to get to finish this argument until I did.

"There's a body."

"A dead body?" I clarified.

Fergie nodded. "Exactly. The insurers want to know if you'll look into it."

"Who died?" I asked Fergie.

"Her name was Jessica Hammersmith."

That name seemed vaguely familiar, but I couldn't place it. I didn't need to. Someone was dead. Presumably, someone who mattered to her family and friends. Probably not in great circumstances if there was enough doubt for the insurers to call me in.

Niall stood there, and suddenly, I couldn't read him. He looked worried though. "Have you investigated many deaths?"

"Not many," I replied. Those I had looked into had been in cases where there had been magical accidents, and the coven didn't want that to be common knowledge. My main job had been ensuring that they just looked like everyday human incompetence.

"I should come with you," Niall said.

I shook my head. "Thanks, but I don't think so."

"It might be dangerous, Elle."

"She's already dead. I think the danger is past." I paused. "Niall, this is my job. I'm not having my boyfriend follow me around on my job, even if the police will allow it. Go ahead and grab lunch on your own and we'll get together for dinner, all right?"

All of which was a valid reason for him not to come. It wasn't the *real* reason, but a good one. The real reason had more to do with the part where we would have to keep this argument going if he stayed with me.

"I will see you tonight," Niall agreed. He kissed me goodbye like it would be our last one. That frightened me just a little. What sort of man worried that every time I left, I might not come back? It was just one more secret for Niall.

* Chapter Five *

By the time I'd driven to the address the insurance company had provided, read an emailed summary of what was going on via my phone and checked with Fergie that the paperwork was in place to do the job, there *wasn't* actually a body. At least, there wasn't one at the scene anymore. Presumably, it was still somewhere, probably at the local morgue. Just not here.

Funnily enough, the police didn't like the idea of leaving dead bodies around for insurance investigators to have a look at. They certainly didn't like the idea of amateurs investigating murders, which had probably disappointed generations of genteel lady sleuths and would-be PIs in this country.

So, there probably wasn't quite as much of a need to rush over to the small house in Craigleith as I made out with Niall around. It was just that I really didn't want to argue any more about my sensibilities when it came to enchantress feeding habits or my moral quandaries when it came to Niall's secrets. Besides there *had* been a body, and that was still important, even if there wasn't one now.

It probably doesn't sound important, sorting out the insurance after a death. Yet, it was more crucial than most people thought. For a family, insurance money could mean the difference between being financially secure and losing their home. It could mean the difference between being able to grieve properly and being buried under a mountain of bills they had no way of paying in the wake of a loved one's death. And in situations where there had been questions raised about a death, it could be even more crucial.

This death had occurred in quite an expensive residential area. Craigleith might have looked normal and suburban, but features like the golf course gave away the truth. It was actually one of the wealthier areas of the city, even the country. Outside of Edinburgh, one had to head down to London and the home counties to find anywhere as flush with money. Craigleith might not have been where the ultra-wealthy like Niall lived, but it was still where plenty of the city's bankers spent their money.

It was a wealthy enough area to suit an up-and-coming musician like Jessica Hammersmith, who had, only a few hours ago, been found dead on her living room floor. I got that from the information Fergie had emailed over. She'd made some money on a surprise single, and was currently a featured singer in a popular subterranean nightclub housed in Edinburgh's Vaults. A hundred years ago, the Vaults had been an infamous underground city full of haunting, murder, and ill repute. Now, they were a tourist attraction. During the Fringe, parts of the Vaults served as the venue for many interesting acts and attracted a lot of counterculture types. She was obviously on the way up.

Beyond that, Fergie had been kind enough to forward me the results of a quick trawl through the search engines, just to let me know what I would be dealing with.

The initial briefing from the insurers told me that the police were not treating the death as suspicious at this stage, but apparently, flags had been raised by those close to the deceased, and the insurers wanted me to make sure that everything was investigated before they made any kind of payout. The insurance policy had a suicide clause—an exception—and of course, it would be to their benefit if Jessica Hammersmith did commit suicide, but with the relatives objecting, they wanted to be sure.

I was the lucky investigator who got the job of either telling them that there probably wouldn't be a payout, or telling them that something even worse had happened to the person they cared about.

I stood on the doorstep, rang the bell, and did my best to prepare myself for what I would probably find within. Not blood, or guts, or gore. The fact that there were no police left guarding the place told me that anything like that was long gone. Even so, there would be a residue left. An imprint of events. A stir. An echo. Even a ghost, if I was really unlucky.

It was a full minute before someone answered the door. The woman who did so was taller than me, with dark hair falling loose to her waist and eyes of such a piercing blue that for a moment, it was impossible to look beyond them. She was beautiful enough that she could have been a model, albeit one on her day off, given that she was wearing jeans, boots and a sweater, although all three looked like they were by designer names.

She also looked like she'd been crying. Not that it seemed to have done anything to mar her looks. "Look, whoever you are, I've told all of you. No interviews. Not now."

"I'm not with the press," I said, holding out my business card. "I'm from the insurance company. I know this must be a difficult time for you, but they want me to look into the death of Jessica Hammersmith."

The woman moved forward, and for a fraction of a second, it looked like I'd managed to say the wrong thing. Like she was going to attack me there and then. I tensed to defend myself, trying to remind myself not to do anything too violent to a human.

Instead of attacking me though, she hugged me tightly, crushing me to her perfumed body, relief pouring off her like summer rain. For a moment, the invisible part of me that hungered for emotion licked metaphorical lips at that potential, but I pushed it down. I had to be professional. I hadn't come here to feed. I had come to investigate. The part of me that never stopped hungering could wait. It wasn't like it was going to go away.

"Thank goodness you're here," the woman said, stepping back to let me inside. "I tried telling the police that Jess would have never…" She trailed off. "They didn't listen."

"I'm sorry," I said. "You have to understand though…"

"Victoria. Victoria de Newe. I was Jess's friend."

"Victoria." I tried to sound as professional as I could. I didn't want to get her hopes up. "I'm here to investigate because you raised suspicions, but I can only follow the facts I find. I don't know what I'm going to be able to find that the police haven't."

"You'll find something," Victoria insisted, "because you won't make all the assumptions about Jess that the police did. Look, come through to the kitchen. I'd say the living room, but…"

But, according to the file, that had been where they'd found Jessica Hammersmith's body. She'd been found hanged, and it had probably been Victoria who found her, if she was the only one here. I could practically taste it in her reaction. The police's opinion of the circumstances was obvious. Just by the fact that there wasn't a forensics team sweeping every inch of this place, it was clear that the police had decided it was a suicide. Not just a suicide, but an open and shut one. People said a lot of things about the police, but one thing I'd found over the years was that when it seemed like there was even a *possibility* of a serious crime, they made sure that they checked. They didn't want to be seen to have ignored something like a possible murder.

Jessica Hammersmith's house was nice enough inside. It was expensively decorated, but with a certain sameness to it that suggested it had been done by an interior decorator. There were a few more homey touches in the form of pictures on the wall, a couple of framed newspaper cuttings, that kind of thing, yet the impression I got was of a place that someone came back to occasionally, rather than a place they lived. One photo caught my eye, of a young woman in her twenties, standing on a stage. She was petite, dark-haired, and pretty. There was something so delicate about her that it was almost ethereal, yet I could almost feel the power of the performance coming through the image.

"Jess's career was just starting to take off," Victoria said as she led the way through to a large kitchen that looked like hardly anyone used it. "She'd only just bought this place, as a way of saying to herself that she'd made it, I guess. She loved to sing, and now people were seeing how special she was. Only… this happened. I can't believe she's gone."

I could feel her fighting to keep her emotions under control, so I sat her down at the kitchen table, found some coffee, and started to make it for both of us.

Victoria took the glass dome off a marbled coffee cake in the center of the table. It was a strangely domestic moment given what had happened here, but if it helped her to feel that things were normal, I could work with it. I cut us each a slice and plated them before getting us forks. She replaced the glass dome. I sat down with her and nibbled on the cake as she spoke.

"There were journalists here earlier, when the police were," Victoria said, out of nowhere. "It's why I thought you might be one. They got a whiff of a story: 'Promising young star takes own life.' I guess that's all Jess will be now. Some tiny story in the local press. Probably not even front page. She'd hate that."

I could feel the regret, along with a tangle of other emotions that felt like more than anything even a friend would have felt. I handed Victoria her coffee. She nodded gratefully.

"You and Jessica were lovers?" I ventured.

Victoria hesitated. "Sometimes. Maybe. It was complicated. It was always complicated, with Jess. She still wasn't sure about a lot of what she wanted. She was worried about what her family would think, they were very High Kirk, and of course, it was all just one more thing for the police to pick up on. As if somehow, two women being lovers would have something to do with Jessica's death."

"Just one more thing?" I asked. "To go with what else?"

Victoria shook her head. "Oh, I told them that Jess had just left her record company, and they assumed that she'd been dumped by them. They found…Jess wasn't into drugs, not seriously, anyway, but in their heads by that point, she was this big rock 'n roll cliché, you know?"

"Fame plus drugs leads to death?" I added.

"That's the picture they painted for themselves before they even finished looking around. I couldn't exactly deny what was next to the b—" She paused. "Isn't it crazy that I can't even say 'the body'? It's not like it changes anything. She's gone."

"I am so sorry, Victoria."

"I can't believe she's gone. She was…so vibrant. So full of energy."

I reached out to touch her hand, lightly. Her emotions welled into me. I stopped after a few moments, realizing that there were some things I shouldn't intrude upon like that. I slowly withdrew my hand from Victoria's.

"I do need to ask, Victoria. What is it that makes you think that Jessica—Jess—didn't kill herself?"

"She wouldn't," Victoria insisted. "It was something she would never do. She was happy. There was no reason for her to even think about killing herself. The record company thing was nothing. It would have blown over with a little gossip for the music industry, but nothing else. Six months from now, Jess could have started her own record company. We were talking about plans for her own label just the other day."

"Interesting." Assuming that was the only reason. Suicide was rarely that simple.

"Miss Chambers, she had so much to live for. Plus, there was no suicide note. The police—"

"I can guess. The police would have said that people don't always leave suicide notes."

Victoria nodded. "That's right."

"Did the police also say that people who are contemplating suicide are also good at hiding what they felt from the people around them?"

"Exactly."

What I didn't say was that some people even seemed happier once they'd decided to go through with their death, because at least that part of their lives was settled. There was no more of the agony of indecision, because they had decided. I knew I couldn't say all of that to Victoria, though. At least not until I'd investigated properly. Not until I was sure.

"I'll need to see where you found her," I told Victoria. "I'll need to know the exact spot. I know it's hard, but do you think you can come in the living room and show me?"

She nodded as though steeling herself, then showed me through to what had probably been a comfortable, modern-styled living room before the Lothian and Borders constabulary had gotten through with it. The furniture was currently pushed back against the walls, while someone had taken the carpet up and removed it, probably because it was ruined or had evidence. Dead bodies tended to leave stains.

"There," Victoria said, waving a hand vaguely in the direction beneath an exposed beam. "I found her there."

"Thank you, Victoria. You don't have to stay in here," I said. "If it's too hard, I'll come through to the kitchen when I'm done. I want to get a… *feel* for what happened here."

Victoria shook her head. "No. This is… this *was* her favorite spot in the house. It feels like I should be here, too, you know? Hanging on to the last little bits of her spirit, if they linger? You understand?"

I nodded. I understood, at least a little. Although it did mean I would have to be a little subtler about what I was doing when I soaked in the last traces of Jessica's emotion in the room. Thankfully, though, my skills weren't exactly of the type that needed a full chalk circle, along with a complete set of unpleasant-looking runes. Although a few of the insurers I'd worked for would probably have sanctioned even those if they thought it would save them money.

"What are you going to do to investigate?" Victoria asked. It was a reasonable-enough question, especially considering the morning she'd probably had. All those police going through the house, probably not explaining anything, would have left her wanting to find some way to keep a grip on the situation.

"First, I'm going to take a look around," I explained casually. "I want to get a feel for who Jessica was, and for what happened here. Is that all right?"

Victoria nodded.

I tried to ask the next question as delicately as I could. "I was called in by the insurers. Are you the main beneficiary of Jessica's insurance policy?"

Victoria shook her head to that one. Apparently, being in the same room where Jessica had died was taking its toll. "Not the main one. I get some, I think, but most of it goes to her family. She has… *had* a little sister."

"Tell me about her little sister."

"Lucy. She's still pretty young. Jess… she was always so good about making sure her sister was taken care of." Victoria sighed heavily. She looked up at me suddenly. "I don't care about her sister getting the money. It's what Jess would have wanted."

I nodded.

"I know why the insurers sent you," Victoria said. "If it was a suicide, they won't pay, right?"

"That is an exemption in most insurance policies," I said, honestly. The least Victoria deserved right then was honesty. "My job is to just gather facts and then I let the insurers decide what to do with them. I'm sorry."

"Talking about Jess in the past tense feels so wrong," Victoria said. "Everything is out of kilter. Everything is gone..." She drifted into soft murmurs that I couldn't quite understand. I could have tried comforting her, but right then, I suspected that the best thing I could do for Victoria was to get on with my job and get out of there.

I tried to tune her out then, focusing on the room. Emotions leave marks on a building. Emotional events with enough power can leave scars deep enough to trap ghosts. And they usually are scars. All too often, the events powerful enough to leave a mark are dark ones. I let my mind settle into the space it needed to feel things in detail... and I caught what I could only describe as an echo.

Hands. Her own hands. The feel of the rope. The despair. The endless, crushing despair. The wish that it would all just stop. That it would just...

I pulled myself back from that echo of Jessica Hammersmith's last moments alive. I'd never had something like that before, thoughts and flashes of physical sensation bound up with the emotion I sensed. It wasn't what I did. Was it something to do with what I'd become? I'd have to ask Niall how to handle this as an enchantress. Had this been why he'd wanted to come along? Had he suspected I might run into something like this? If so, he could have *said* something.

Of course, I might not have listened.

For now though, there was one certainty in this room where a promising young musician and performer had died. Jessica Hammersmith hadn't been anywhere near as happy as Victoria thought. Everything I could feel from the echo of the moments of death pointed to her killing herself. I could feel it in the air. The darkness. The hurt.

But there was something more to it, something so dark, so evil and so heartbreaking that...

Suddenly, I had to get out of that room. *I had to.*

"I-I'm just going to look upstairs," I said hurriedly.

"Upstairs?" Victoria looked at me blankly.

"To get a feel for Jessica's life. I want to see the spaces where she spent time."

That seemed to be good enough for Victoria, although she still watched me like a mother hen as I went around the upper part of the house, obviously worried that I would damage something precious to Jessica, or take something, a souvenir from a rich and almost-famous person.

The truth was simpler: it was as far as I could get from the living room without actively running from the house.

In Jessica's bedroom, I found scrapbooks and more pictures. They held flashes of happier emotions, enough to bring me out from under the lingering effects of the weighty depression in the living room.

Yet, I knew I was just using that to distract myself from what I needed to do. Turning over photos of Jessica Hammersmith on stage or meeting real stars didn't change anything.

She was still just as dead as she had been earlier.

Her happiness had been as beautiful as she had been, but it didn't change what I'd felt downstairs. I ought to tell Victoria that the person she so obviously loved *had* killed herself.

Except that then, I *felt* it. I didn't notice it at first because it was so subtle, and because frankly, it was a feeling I was used to feeling every day. A faint, but familiar, taste mixed in with the rest of everything there that had no place in that room. There had been another emotional vampire in the house. One whose power I could sense, clinging like smoke as it drifted over everything Jessica Hammersmith owned.

* Chapter Six *

The last time I'd gone to see Siobhan up near Arthur's Seat in the middle of Holyrood Park, her goblin boyfriend had tried to attack me. I wasn't physically afraid of Dougie now, but it was still a fact that had me looking around cautiously as I waited for her, wanting to make sure that she showed up alone.

If she showed up at all. After all, it had taken long enough over the phone to convince her to come. She'd been sure I was planning trouble for her over the theft earlier. Apparently, despite her certainty about me not involving the coven, she didn't completely get that insurance investigators had better things to do than bring in goblins for stealing from tourists. Maybe she thought I was still angry about the petty cash. Maybe she was even right.

So, I stood there waiting for her, looking out over the city from the vantage point of the monument. It was a clear day, so the Scottish Parliament Building was kind of hard to miss, all sweeping curves reflecting the sunlight as it tried to emphasize the importance of the politicians within.

I tried calling Niall while I waited for Siobhan, but I didn't get through. That was unusual. Normally, he picked up pretty quickly for me, regardless of what else he was doing. Although I guessed I hadn't been with Niall long enough to really know what was normal with him when it came to anything.

I didn't have the time to think about it more though, because Siobhan chose that moment to arrive. She sloped up the path from the monument, just one of the ways into the goblins' world of tunnels and darkness. I could feel a kind of sullen unhappiness coming off her, along with a hint of something close to fear. Not a promising mood to begin a meeting with. Still, at least Dougie wasn't with her. This time, we were going to have some one-on-one time. That was good. Without Dougie around, I liked Siobhan.

"Siobhan, hi." I tried to project a little more friendliness and relaxation. Something to tone down the mood a little. "Thanks for coming."

Siobhan fiddled with the hood of her top. The sunlight was still obviously a little strong for her. That was a pity. I knew how much she liked being out from Underneath.

"Are you doing all right?" I asked. "Are you hungry? Do you want to go get a cup of coffee with me or something?"

"Thanks, but food isn't too appealing right now." She put her weight on one foot and then the other, obviously impatient to cut things short. "You said you needed information. And…I didn't get my pay from the other day. Because of everything that happened."

Information meant money. I held out a small roll of cash. Siobhan took it, making it disappear into a pocket with the kind of speed that said more about her as a thief and pickpocket than about any particular goblin abilities. Even that wasn't enough to make her cloud of unhappiness dissipate completely, though.

Whatever it was, it would have to wait. I had my own problems right then. "Siobhan, I need to know about vampires."

"So, shouldn't you be asking that rich boyfriend of yours?" the goblin girl shot back.

I would, if he ever got around to answering his phone. "I don't have a lot of patience today, Siobhan," I warned her. "I didn't have to let you go earlier. I could have held you there and called for the police."

"No…I…" I could feel the little flicker of guilt there, and embarrassment.

"I need to know if you've heard about any vampires in Edinburgh."

"Besides you and Niall?" Siobhan asked, half-turning away.

I reached out, pulling her back toward me. Maybe a little faster than I should have, because her hood slipped slightly, leaving her blinking against the light. It also gave me a pretty clear view of the bruises covering one side of her face.

"Siobhan!" I said. I couldn't keep the shock out of my voice.

"It's nothing," she said, dragging her hood up again hastily.

I could feel that lie for what it was. "Did Dougie do that?"

"It's not his fault."

"Of course it's his fault! If he did it, it's his fault." I reached out to put my hand on her arm. "You should walk away, Siobhan. Just leave him. He's not good enough for you. He is dragging you down with every decision he makes about his own life, and you are letting him decide for you too by staying with him."

"I love him, Elle. And it's complicated."

She was the second person today to tell me that her relationship was complicated. I shook my head. "Not from where I'm standing. You're still young. You don't know how things are."

"You're the one standing in the sun," Siobhan snapped back. "What am I meant to do? Leave the tunnels? Come up here and slowly fry? I love the up-world. I love it as much as any goblin can, but I still can't live up here. I'm sorry about the petty cash from your office and breaking into it to…sleep together. I know that was wrong. We just wanted a place to go and be alone. I love him, Elle."

I sighed. "Oh, Siobhan. You can't be with him. He's destroying you."

"Leave it, Elle. Please, just leave it."

Again, I was all too aware that I could have made her come with me. I could have pushed emotions into Siobhan to make her get away from Dougie. Even made her stop loving him, given time. I could have done all those things, and every one of them would have been evil. Even when I thought they were the right things for Siobhan. Maybe especially then. Regardless of what I was, I didn't get to make those kinds of decisions for other people. There had to be a stopping point, or what was I?

I asked what I'd come up there for again, instead. "Vampires, Siobhan. Enchanters. Whatever they want to call themselves. Are there any in Edinburgh besides me and Niall?"

Siobhan shook her head. "Not any that I know about."

"You're sure?"

"I just said it, didn't I?" There was an edge to her voice that was clearly designed to shut the conversation down. Well, of course she was going to be angry with me, after I'd just told her to dump her boyfriend.

Unfortunately, I couldn't leave it like that. "It's important, Siobhan. I need to be certain. It is a matter of life and death. Are there any other enchanters in Edinburgh?"

Siobhan shrugged. "I don't know about any. If I hear anything…"

Which was the other reason I couldn't push Siobhan into coming with me. Down in the dark of the goblins' world, she could find out things that I couldn't. She could maybe hear something that would point me in the direction of the killer. Up here, she might be safer, but she couldn't help me. Not everything that was dark and evil hid down in the depths where Siobhan lived, but enough things did that I needed to know about them.

"All right, thank you," I said, heading off down the hill, past some of the trees that lined the way. I took out my phone again, trying Niall once more. This time, I got through.

"Elle?"

"Niall, is everything okay, you sound—"

"It's fine," he assured me. He paused for a second. "I'm sorry about this morning."

"So am I. I need to talk to you. It's about the case I'm working on."

Another pause. Face to face, I might have had some sense of the reason for it, but over the phone, there was nothing.

"Can it wait?" Niall asked. "I'm in the middle of something."

"This is a murder, Niall," I said.

"And I will help all I can, but this is…business."

"What kind of business?" I asked. He seemed to have so much business, so many deals going on at once. It was another area of his life where it felt like Niall hadn't let me in completely yet.

"A meeting. One I cannot put off. I will call you as soon as it is done, I promise. And Elle?"

"Yes?" I couldn't keep some of the exasperation out of my voice.

"I love you."

"I love you, too," I said, although I accompanied it with a sigh as I hung up.

Which was exactly when someone started shooting at me.

I didn't hear the first shot, but I felt something whisper past my cheek, and I saw the mess that was all that was left of the bark on the tree behind me. It probably said a lot about both my life and the country in which I live that my first thought wasn't "gun." Instead, what got me scrambling for cover behind the tree was the memory of a couple of magical attacks in my recent past; there had been ones that had sent me flying back into objects and smashed through walls. I didn't want a repeat performance.

I ducked back behind the tree, and as I did so, another bullet slammed into it. This time, there was no mistaking what it was. Someone was actually *shooting* at me. I hadn't seen anyone else around. I hadn't heard anything, either. A sniper with a suppressed rifle. Who would have something like that in Scotland? Actually, the answer to that probably covered a whole host of people, from ghillies up on the big estates in the Highlands down.

Thankfully, so far, neither the gun nor the shooter had proven to be very accurate. Probably not a ghillie, then, or a professional sniper. Either of those would have hit me the first time. Certainly, the second time. I almost laughed at how calmly my brain could supply me with that thought, although I stopped laughing soon enough when another bullet flew by the tree and thunked into the tree behind me.

What were my options? Call the police and hunker down behind cover until they came? Make a run for it? Try to take the offensive? I couldn't take the first option, partly because I might be dead before they arrived, but mostly because the only reasons I could think of for someone shooting at me had far too much to do with the supernatural to risk involving the human police. Of course, the shooter probably wouldn't want to risk them either, so they would probably be repositioning even as I thought about it, looking for a line of sight…

I stretched out my senses, and I felt something on me. The soft weight of someone's attention. The tiny certainty that I was being looked at. Specifically, I sensed the cold, clear emotion of someone staring right at the center of my chest. I threw myself flat just in time, hearing the shot go overhead. I scrambled behind the tree again, knowing that it wouldn't help me for long.

I tried to get a grip on the attention I had felt, reaching out with my talents, and found it after a second or two of searching. It was a thin beam of concentration, almost laser-like in its intensity, the focus of someone looking down a telescopic sight at one spot, waiting for me to so much as glance out from behind my hiding place.

At least, if I went out to my right. Instead, I went left, making it to the next tree before my would-be assassin could shift his aim. I felt for the beam of concentration as it flicked back and forth, trying to time the movements. This time, I skidded into the next patch of cover only an instant before a bullet went past. I heard it sing by and shuddered. That was too close. I needed to change tactics.

So, I did. A month ago, I wouldn't have had any options left. A month ago, I had thought I was weak. Far weaker than any other witch. Now I knew that all those spells I'd spent my life trying to learn weren't as out of reach as I'd once thought.

On the night we had finally slept together, Niall had shown me that by conjuring a witch light that I'd been sure was impossible for an enchanter. I'd been wrong. All I'd needed was the right emotional fuel.

There wasn't a lot of energy in the beam of concentration, but there was something. Better yet, it gave me a clear line back to the shooter. I scooped it up, drank it in, and whispered what I could remember of the words to a spell designed to conjure lightning. The spark that formed in my hands wasn't much, but I threw it anyway, flinging it back along the beam that sought me out.

As the cry came behind me, I ran. The bolt wouldn't be strong enough to kill. It probably wouldn't even be strong enough to stun someone for long, but a spark of lightning to the eye was still something. So I ran, not bothering to even try to find out who was shooting at me. I already had a pretty good idea of who in Edinburgh had the resources to send a gunman after me.

Which was why I ran down from Arthur's Seat, heading down into the city, not going home, but instead, heading for a very familiar set off offices. The walk took me perhaps twenty minutes, and most of that I spent trying not to shake too much at the thought of what had just happened. Someone had tried to shoot me.

I could have done a lot of things then. I could have called Niall and waited while he took the kind of revenge that only he could. I could have called Fergie, and dealt with things through the long, slow processes of the law. I could have grabbed a bag and left the city, finally accepting that it was too dangerous for me to stay in Edinburgh.

I didn't do any of those things.

Rebecca was just coming out of her small coven sub-office when I arrived, looking every inch as blonde and businesslike as she always did. I didn't hesitate. Instead, I strode over, pushing her back against the nearest wall, my forearm at her throat. She gasped and started the movements of a spell but I increased the pressure.

"You know that won't work. If you fight me, it will only cost you the energy you've been working so hard to rebuild after last time."

She stopped. Clearly, she could see that I was serious. "Elle? What are you—"

"Someone just shot at me, Rebecca."

"Shot at you? And you just naturally assumed that it was me? First of all, you have no right—"

"I have every right."

I could feel the indignation pouring off her, and the fear underneath it. Was she involved? It made sense if she was. The coven had plenty of reasons to fear me. Rebecca, especially.

"A couple of hours ago, I opened an investigation about a dead body. One that had traces of one of my kind all around it. Suddenly, I have people shooting at me? Who do I know who hates enchantresses, who has access to trained killers, and who would just be looking for an excuse to decide we were too dangerous to live, hmm?"

Rebecca shook her head furiously, unable to say anything as I slightly increased the pressure on her throat. She looked like she was on the verge of panic. Maybe that had something to do with the levels of anger that were leaking out of me just then. Maybe it just had something to do with her lack of air. Yet, she didn't *feel* guilty to me, not the way I would have expected if she'd ordered someone to shoot me. I relaxed my grip, just a little.

"I didn't do it," Rebecca said, gasping. "I promise you, Elle. I didn't."

"Yes, well, we both know what your promises are worth," I said, but I let go of her. "If I find out that you're going back on our truce agreement, Rebecca, you know what I'll do."

"You'll drain me," Rebecca said, the words coming out quietly. She swallowed a small sound of fear.

I stared at her for a moment or two, letting that sink in. The trouble was, I was sure it wasn't her by now. Although maybe she could still help me.

"Maybe later. For now, I want information. Are there any other enchantresses anywhere near Edinburgh?"

Rebecca shook her head. "Not that the coven knows about. We keep track where we can."

"I'll just bet you do. Mostly waiting for a chance to kill us." I turned to walk away, but I wasn't feeling as kindly toward her as I had with Siobhan. "If you think of anything, you'd better let me know."

"Well, there's one thing I know," Rebecca shot back. "If someone has been killed by a vampire and it wasn't you, there's only one suspect."

I didn't turn and drain her just for saying it. I was actually quite proud of my restraint.

"There's more than that, Elle." She didn't feel like she wanted to tell me this part. "I've been thinking about coming to you with it, but…"

"But it wouldn't do to be seen working with me," I supplied. "Oh, and you thought I might eat you."

Rebecca hesitated, but then said it. Quietly, but she said it. She really was terrified of me. I wasn't sure whether I liked that or not.

"Yes. And… people have been disappearing. I mean, there are always people who go missing but this…it's more than usual, and the people…"

"What about them?"

"They're all witches. Witches and warlocks. Barely, in some cases. Minor talents. But they're all ours, and they're all missing. *Recently* missing."

Which explained another part of why she hadn't come to me with it. She was worried I might be behind it.

"What?" I said. "You think that I'm on some kind of magic eating binge? You think I did this?"

"You have every reason to be angry with the coven," Rebecca said, "and you have already explained on several occasions exactly what you would do to me if—"

"Because you tried to *kill* me!" I snapped back. "That doesn't mean that I'm suddenly taking people off the street just for having magic."

I started to walk away again.

"Elle, if it's not you, it's Niall," Rebecca said. I stopped, and she kept going. "You know it, and I know it. This death of yours, definitely. And who else has a reason to go after our people? So, the only question is what you're going to do about it. Or are you going to wait for the coven to do it for you?"

I did spin then, pinning her to the wall without having to use my hands, letting a wash of fear do the work for me. "You do not touch Niall. Not again. Not ever."

"N-not even if he's the k-killer?" Rebecca somehow managed, even through the fear.

I didn't dignify that with an answer. Mostly because I didn't have one myself.

* Chapter Seven *

"Did you get the petty cash back?" Fergie asked, when I got back to the office after seeing Siobhan.

"Dougie spent it," I said. "It's not like Siobhan knew about the theft. How did the goblins get in the office last night? Did you figure that out?"

I knew I was only putting off the moment when I would have to talk about the things that mattered, but some things were worth putting off. I'd already let Fergie know the basics of what had happened at Jessica Hammersmith's house. It was enough for now that he knew.

"I sniffed them back to the ductwork, traced it down to the cellar of the building, and there's a spot where the cellar connects to tunnels below."

So, my office was connected to the goblins' tunnels. Great. "Nice detective work, Fergie."

"You're welcome," he said. "It helps to have the nose of a werewolf. I've screwed down the access panel in the cellar more securely and have padlocked things for now. I've changed the door code as you requested. I have a couple of contractors coming the day after tomorrow to give you bids for installing steel security grates inside the ductwork."

"Good decision."

He nodded. "We can't let goblins come in here…they like to take my food."

The truth was that I wasn't too worried about the food. The less haggis there was in the office, the better, from where I was standing. On the other hand, I didn't like the idea that anyone could just walk into my personal space like that without my knowledge. Especially not when I had just been shot at.

I spent much of the rest of the day going through paperwork in the office. Maybe it wasn't the most efficient way to catch a supernatural killer, but I couldn't afford to miss anything. I wanted to be the first to know about anything in Jessica Hammersmith's life that might give me the identity of her killer. At least, that's what I told myself while Fergie and I were going through her insurance documents and everything we could find online about the former rising star.

Jessica Hammersmith had certainly been able to sing. I got that part from watching a few old YouTube clips of her on stage. More than that, she'd had a real stage presence. That indefinable something that made it seem like she was making a connection with every member of the audience, even in early gigs that were too small to be worth a mention. Her official website pointed to a new album close to being released, which might now be put out as a tribute to her, while her social network feeds had attracted the usual swarm of messages of condolence in the wake of her death. And speculation as well. How had Jessica Hammersmith really died? Thousands of fans wanted to know.

"Did you track down the beneficiaries of the insurance policy?" I asked Fergie.

My werewolf legal advisor nodded. "A sister out near Queensferry is the main beneficiary, although there's a small provision for a Ms. V. de Newe. I managed to track down Ms. Hammersmith's solicitors, too, and while they obviously wouldn't give me details, an old acquaintance of mine there was at least prepared to hint that there wouldn't be any surprises in the will."

"So, there will be no leaving everything to a convenient third party?" I suggested.

Fergie shook his head and cleared his throat. "Elle. Please don't take this the wrong way, but only in the spirit of concern in which I intend it…"

He had my attention now.

"At what point are you just going to walk up to Niall and ask him if he did this?"

I took a deep breath and let it out. "Leave it, Fergie."

He shrugged. "You know as well as I do that Niall—"

"I said leave it." I was firm that time.

He left it. Clearly, he didn't want to be an *unemployed* werewolf legal advisor. Of course, I knew what he was saying: all this was little better than a distraction. We both knew that, with only two vampires like me in Edinburgh, if I hadn't been around Jessica, then Niall had. If I had any sense, I would confront him about that. I should probably confront him about the missing people, too.

That didn't mean I had to do it, though

"Do you have another theory?" Fergie asked me. "I mean, if there's anything better, fine."

I shrugged. "What about if the coven set this up as a way to find an excuse for getting rid of Niall?"

Fergie considered it. "Could they fake the presence of an enchanter? Could they set this up? Why would they go to the trouble?"

"You said yourself that there are indications they're building up to something."

"Yes, but that doesn't necessarily mean anything for this."

"I also just saw Rebecca."

"You didn't tell me that," Fergie said.

"I'm the boss. I don't have to tell you everything." I took a deep breath and met his eyes. "Someone shot at me with a suppressed rifle today."

"They did *what?*" Fergie might have been a werewolf, but that didn't automatically make him some kind of tough guy. He was, at heart, still a lawyer. Lawyers didn't live in a world where people they knew got shot at.

"While I was on the phone with Niall. Which is why I went to see Rebecca. I figured that if anyone was going to start shooting at me…"

Fergie swallowed. "You didn't do anything to her, did you?"

I shook my head. "Don't think I wasn't tempted though. She thought Niall was the killer. She also started telling me that witches and warlocks had been disappearing. She thought it might be me."

"Elle, this is not good. Not good at all." Fergie tapped his pen on a legal pad, thinking, his brows knitting together.

"I know it's not good. Too many things are happening, too fast. What I need is advice. Is there anyone it could be besides Niall?"

"You've already mentioned the coven," Fergie said. "I guess the question is one of who else stands to gain. I know the insurance company doesn't have to pay out if this is suicide."

"You're even going to suspect them now?" I asked.

"You wanted possibilities. I didn't say they were good possibilities. Sorry."

No, because whatever else had happened, I had felt an enchanter in Jessica's home. I still needed to find out what that meant.

"Look into the people who have disappeared," I said to Fergie. "Find out what you can about them. I don't like Rebecca suddenly dropping something like that on me. I'll concentrate on the main case for now."

"You think that they're linked?" Fergie asked.

"I don't know." I hoped not. Because the only way I could see that they might be linked was if Rebecca was right. If Niall was behind all of it. I couldn't believe that. Not yet. Not until I saw some *proof*.

I didn't so much as mention the case to Niall when I went to his place. I didn't even mention the near-shooting, in case it sent him on some kind of hunt for the coven. For his part, Niall was quiet, too, not bringing up the business he'd been caught up in all day. He just played the piano for a while in the living room, old tunes that I didn't really recognize. He was so intent on playing that I wasn't sure that he even noticed the moment when I left to go back to my place. It made me a little sad. Under the weight of suspicion, we were losing… *us*.

The next morning brought me back to the office through the press of street performers already out touting for their bigger shows later that day. Fergie was already at his desk when I arrived. That was only to be expected. The woman sitting across from him was more of a surprise.

"Victoria?"

She turned as I said it, looking every bit as perfect as she had on Jessica Hammersmith's doorstep. She smiled up at me from one of the client chairs. "Elle, hi. I hope you don't mind me coming here like this. It's just…well, you're looking into what happened, and I thought maybe you'd want to see these."

She passed me a trio of business cards. They were for clubs.

"Places where Jessica sang?" I asked.

Victoria shook her head. "I don't think so. Maybe. I don't know. It's just…they weren't with any of the other business things. Jess was normally pretty good about that sort of thing. She had these sort of…hidden."

Victoria was worried by that thought. I could feel that much.

"What is it?" I asked.

"It's probably nothing," Victoria said. "I'm probably just being foolish."

"But?"

"But one of them kind of has a…reputation. As a singles' bar, you know?" Victoria shook her head. "I don't know why I'm even telling you this. It feels like I'm being disloyal even thinking it, but what if it had something to do with what happened and I didn't say something?"

I knew that feeling. I knew how much it hurt, too. What did you do when the person you loved was keeping secrets? What did you do when you suspected that there were things about them that you had never known?

"I'll look into it," I promised, and not just because I wanted to make Victoria feel better. The slight flicker of a smile that crossed her features was just a bonus. A bonus that reminded me I hadn't fed in a couple of days. And if I was noticing that around women, I was getting *really* hungry.

I forced myself to focus as Fergie showed Victoria to the door.

"So, you're going to look at these places?" he asked.

"If Jessica was looking for another relationship, then that could explain how she met the enchanter I felt in her house," I explained. "It could be that they stalked her there."

"Stalked? This isn't some 1950s' horror movie."

I shrugged. "Said the werewolf to the emotional vampire. If we're lucky, someone at one of these places will remember Jessica. If we're really lucky, they'll remember *who* she met there."

"It does sound like the perfect place for an enchanter to hunt," Fergie admitted. He looked at me. "Are you going to be okay? Marie says you've been careful about feeding."

That caught me by surprise. Both because of the idea of Niall's personal assistant talking to Fergie about that, and because of the flash of affection that came with her name.

"You and Marie have a thing? Is there something I should know?" I asked.

Fergie shook his head. "Not so far. Maybe. And you're changing the subject."

"I'll be fine," I assured him. "Unless you're volunteering to be my lunch?"

"Unless you're planning on turning furry with the full moon and howling on all fours, we couldn't do the open wound thing to get you fed. That leaves kissing, so, I don't think it would be me who would have the issue with it, would it?"

He had a point. As good looking as Fergie was, I'd already written off that possibility, and I wasn't going to kiss him just to feed. Let alone anything else.

"I think I'd better stick to less furry food."

Fergie laughed. "I've never felt so safe."

I went home early. Obviously, this was going to be a nighttime job, so there was no point in exhausting myself in the office while I waited. I tried to do research on vampires, on Jessica, on anything that would distract me, but mostly, I ended up thinking about Niall. Oh, and sleeping. Somehow, I ended up sleeping through most of the day. Maybe it was the lack of energy.

I was still running on an empty stomach, emotionally speaking, when I finally grabbed a few things and headed out to try to find answers. I was dressed in a black party dress, a leather jacket, and heels. The kind of outfit that would normally have gotten me attention, but seemed right for the places I was heading. The hunger wasn't so bad once I got out into the street. In fact, it was part of why I walked. There were enough performers around that I could at least let the emotion of the watching crowds run through me. It didn't do anything to solve the underlying problem, but it was something. The same taste, until…

Until what? The problem of needing to feed wasn't going to go away. The problem of what I needed to *do* to feed wasn't going to go away. Maybe I could rely on Niall's staff for a little while longer, and maybe I would be able to persuade him to give me more energy, but that only postponed the issue. Besides, did I really want to think about where Niall might have gotten his energy from? Who he might have gotten it from? The things Rebecca had said were still in the background. Had Jessica Hammersmith had some minor magical talent? Was there any way to check? If she did, did it prove anything?

I shook my head. For now, I needed to focus on the clubs. The first one seemed to be a general venue, currently advertising a comedy revue and a one-woman show. There wasn't a line outside, but that was typical. For every bestselling show at the Fringe, there were three more that only attracted maybe enough people to fill one table. I walked inside, paying the cover charge and then looking for the manager.

She turned out to be a woman maybe a decade older than me, heavily built, with the kind of harassed look that probably only came from trying to run a venue in the middle of the Fringe.

"I'm afraid we're busy at the moment," she said as I tried to talk to her.

I looked around pointedly at the nearly empty venue, and then held up a picture of Jessica taken from her website. "I'm here about this woman."

"I don't know her."

I sighed. I'd been hoping to do this without using my talents, but now I sent a tendril of persuasive power into her. "Could you maybe look at the picture before you say that?"

She took the photo. "I'm sorry, I really don't recognize her. I mean, with the crowds that come through the city…"

I nodded. "But this is a club where a lot of single people come?"

She frowned slightly. "Not really. Although we did have a speed dating thing maybe a month ago."

Speed dating. That was something, and it turned out with just a little more pushing that they'd kept the sign-up sheets. Which they obviously couldn't show to anyone, but since it was me…Jessica's name was there, about halfway through the pile. From the looks of it, she'd gotten a lot of responses. I wasn't surprised. Niall's name wasn't there, but did that prove anything other than that he would be smart enough to use a false name?

I moved on to the next club. The moment I arrived, I knew that this one was different. I could feel it, even from the street. Need, desire, pleasure, it all poured out of the doors in a wave. A month ago, I would have locked down my shields and walked away at the feel of it, but now, I eagerly stepped inside. There was a line. The bouncers didn't make me join it. They didn't remember Jessica, either, when I asked.

Inside, the club was full, and not just with people there to enjoy the music. I could feel the straightforward wants of everyone in the room, pulsing out as clearly as the dubstep coming from the speakers. Although I wasn't completely out of place, and there were plenty of "normally" dressed people there, there were also plenty of people wearing a lot more leather than me. Or a lot less, in a few cases.

I got at least three offers on the way to the bar, each of a kind that suggested there was more to the club than just a place to meet. I could even feel it if I tried. There were things going on somewhere up a broad staircase to the rear of the club that both made me want to walk away and made unseen parts of me groan in anticipation. I forced myself to ignore them as I pushed Jessica's picture at a barman who seemed, like most of the bar staff, to have temporarily misplaced his shirt. Not that I was complaining, given his physique.

"Have you seen this woman?" I asked.

"Now, you know we'd go out of business if we went around telling people that their partners were here," he said with a smile.

I shook my head and pushed him, just slightly, before asking my question again.

"Yes," he said. "Okay, she *was* here, but it's my job if anyone finds out I told you like this."

I could feel the nerves coming off him. I could also feel everything he felt when he looked at me. It was a delicious combination. Almost without thinking about it, I reached forward, hooked an arm around his neck, and kissed him. I kissed him, and as I did, just a sliver of those emotions slid down into me.

"For risking your job for me," I said as I pulled back, although it didn't seem like enough then. Maybe I should go back and find one of the people who had come up to me? Maybe I should just grab someone from the crowd? It wasn't like they would say no, if I suggested that we should check out what was going on upstairs. And I wouldn't be much of an investigator if I left a whole area of the club uninvestigated...

I was actually, honestly, seriously considering it when I felt the lightest of touches on my arms. I knew who it was even before I turned. Even through the emotional noise of the club, I could feel him.

"Niall, what are you doing here?" It was just one of the questions I wanted to ask, but it seemed like as good a place as any to begin.

He answered me with a kiss. If he was trying to compete with the bartender's kiss, Niall won, hands down. Well, hands up, and around, and just generally all over me. His tongue darted inside my mouth, and I felt my energy joining with his as the kiss turned more than physical. Eventually though, he pulled back.

"Come on," he said softly. "I want to take you home and undress you slowly."

When he put it like that, all the other questions I had didn't seem so important.

* Chapter Eight *

As it turned out, Niall was serious about undressing me slowly. We had raced back to his place in his Aston Martin, probably breaking a number of traffic regulations along the way, only for him to slow things down once we finally reached his bedroom. Instead of pushing me back onto the vast expanse of his Egyptian cotton sheets, he had me stand beside the bed, very still while he started to peel me out of my clothing.

He made a slow string of kisses on my skin, his lips following every movement his hands made. They brushed against my neck as he took my jacket from me, working down to my shoulders in a wave of butterfly touches. They traced a line of heat down my back as he unzipped my dress, inch by maddening inch.

There were questions I wanted to ask. Questions I needed answers to. I even tried to get them out as Niall's lips moved back up to my shoulders, his hands pulling away the shoulder straps of my dress so that the dark material slid down and pooled on the floor.

"Niall, what were you doing in the club?"

"Watching over you," he whispered against my skin. "Do you really want to talk now, Elle?"

I was about to point out that we'd hardly talked in the last couple of days, but then his hands moved over me and I forgot all about talking. His lips kept up that slow, teasing movement following his hands, tracing every inch of newly uncovered flesh with his mouth. When Niall unclasped my bra, his tongue moved in lazy circles around my nipples, making me gasp. When he sat me down on the bed and removed my shoes, he kissed his way up to my ankle, finding all the most sensitive spots on my foot. When he finally pulled my panties away from me…

"Oh God, Niall!"

"You like that?" he teased, looking up my body at me before continuing until I couldn't think. Could barely bring myself to move.

"Giving in to what you are has its advantages," Niall murmured, standing and undressing. I watched every moment of it, the way I always did with him. I loved watching that athletic, dancer's body appearing bit by beautiful bit. "Giving in to me has its advantages."

Even feeling as good as I did right then, I wasn't about to allow him that one. When he moved forward to join me on the bed, I flipped Niall onto his back, pinning him down, my hands catching his.

"I never said anything about giving in."

He laughed in delight. "Sharing myself with you as you explore what it is to be an enchantress is an utter joy."

I smiled and felt his warmth and passion rise up. Kissing him, I reached down to take hold of the hard length of him and guide it into me. I sat up, reveling in the moment, moving slowly, and making Niall wait. If he wanted to play games with me, well, I could play them just as well. Finally, though, I felt the pleasure building up within me again, and I couldn't hold back any longer. I moved faster, harder, spilling us both over the edge at the same time.

For the longest time, I lay sprawled over Niall, not wanting to move. Not wanting to lose this moment as he gently stroked my hair. Not wanting to say anything. This worked. Whatever else was complicated between us, *this* worked.

"I am glad you went to that club," Niall whispered after a little while.

"You're glad? I almost—"

"Oh, I am glad that I pulled you out of there in time. It is far better to have you here with me. Far more pleasant."

That was one way of putting it.

"But?" I asked.

"But I am happy that you have finally given in enough to feed the right way," Niall said softly. "It will make things easier. I promise you."

I rolled away from him enough to sit up. "Is that what this is? You're happy that I fed on the bartender? You saw that and you're okay with it?"

Niall took my hand, kissing the inside of my wrist. "You are what you are. I am what I am, too. Should I fault you for being true to your nature?"

"So, you're completely okay with me kissing another guy?"

Niall kissed a little further up my arm. "Did it mean anything? Did this stranger have your heart? Do you suddenly love him? Was it more than just taking the energy you needed? I'd feel jealous then, I promise you."

I shook my head. "You say it like it's nothing. Like it's okay that we just *take*."

Niall had reached my shoulder by now. "We give, too. Or do you think the man you kissed won't think of that moment with pleasure?"

"That isn't the point," I said. "What were you doing in the club? This time, tell me the truth. Tell me *something*."

Niall paused, which was more than a little distracting, because his mouth had just found my ear.

"I was revisiting the past, going back into things that I had thought long buried. I do not want to drag you down into them. I wouldn't want to see your face as I told you about them."

"You said that what matters is whether I love you," I countered. "How can I love you if I don't even really know you? Talk to me."

He sighed, his lips meeting mine halfway through, so that the sound seemed to be inside me. "Tomorrow, Elle. Tomorrow, I will tell you."

"Why not now?"

His hand moved up my thigh. "Because I can think of better things to do with you right now."

Even while I wanted to scream in frustration at him not talking, I had to agree. They *were* better.

I woke with the sunlight streaming down on me. What did it say that I didn't even feel a disconnection at waking up somewhere other than my own bed anymore? And that it still didn't mean I got to wake up beside the man I loved? I looked around, feeling the absence beside me, and then swore. Niall was gone. As usual. I reached out, looking for him with my magic, trying to feel the emotional signature that might mean he was just downstairs. *Nothing.*

I got up, showered, and dressed. Kelly the housekeeper had breakfast waiting for me, and I ate it, even though it wasn't food I wanted right then. It wasn't even energy. It was answers. What had Niall been talking about last night? What parts of the past had been coming back? He'd left early because he'd known I would want answers, I was sure. This wasn't just whatever strange need he had to never be there when I woke. Even so, when Niall's assistant Marie came in to get coffee, I decided to make certain of it.

"Marie, did Niall leave a note for me or anything?" I asked.

She shook her head. "I don't think so. I haven't been over to his study yet, but he would have left something like that where you might find it, wouldn't he?"

"I guess."

"I could check."

I stood up. "No, I'll go."

"I'm really not sure if—"

I cut her off with a look. "I'll go," I repeated, and then forced myself to smile. "Why don't you phone Fergie or something? You know he's interested in you, right?"

Marie's look was surprised, but also pleased. It looked like I'd said the right thing. Good. I didn't always get things right with Niall's staff. I'd probably caused them more than a few problems over the last few weeks. Helping Marie and Fergie was the least I could do. It also meant that Marie was too busy to follow after me. I could be manipulative when I needed to be.

I headed off through the house, looking for Niall's study. I hadn't actually been in there before, because we tended to split our time between the living room, the kitchen, the gallery, and the bedroom. Mostly the bedroom, come to think of it. It didn't take me long to find his study, though.

Given that Niall was born in 1873, I suppose I should have expected the room to look as it did. It was oak paneled, with the same antique furniture found throughout the house. Victorian carved bookcases lined the walls, and there was even a grandfather clock ticking away somberly to itself in the corner. I checked Niall's desk, just in case he really had left a note for me.

He hadn't, but what I found there was almost as interesting. There was a folder, and there was a trinket box. The folder turned out to be full of the details of old agreements, mixed in with letters, most of which seemed to be from women. Several of them referred to gifts the writers hoped that Niall had received.

The tortoise shell and lacquer work trinket box didn't look like much, but I could feel the emotion swirling around it. *Niall's emotion.* Clearly, the contents of the box were important. It was locked, but it was a simple thing for me to take some of the emotion around me and form it into the shape of an unlocking spell.

I opened up the box and sorted through the contents. Some of them were press clippings, obviously taken from very old newspapers. Most of them talked about accidental or unexpected deaths in locations as far afield as Paris and Toronto. There were a couple of small pieces of jewelry, along with a photograph that looked like it had been taken back in the 1920s, judging by the way Niall was dressed. The woman with him looked elegant in black and white, a hat half obscuring her features.

"Elle, did you find what you needed?" Marie called from outside the door. Quickly, I locked everything up again and went out to her.

"Yes," I said. There was no point in taking it out on Marie. "I think I did."

I left then, needing to talk to someone about this, but knowing that it couldn't be with Niall's assistant. I liked

Marie, but she owed Niall her loyalty, not me. It wouldn't be fair to her to ask.

I headed to work, still in my clubbing dress, still attracting fewer stares than I might normally have done, thanks to all the tourists on the streets. For all they knew, the way I was dressed was normal for Edinburgh during the Fringe. As I walked, I tried to think. What did I make of what I'd found? The files? The photo? The truth was that I didn't know. Why would Niall have clippings about sudden deaths? Who had made all those gifts to him?

I still didn't have any answers I liked by the time I reached the office. Fergie was already there, looking pretty happy with himself this morning. Apparently, Marie had phoned him.

"Did you say something to Marie this morning?" he asked softly, as I passed his desk.

I smiled. "Who? Me?"

The other figure there was one I hadn't expected. Siobhan sat waiting for me, her hood down to reveal the odd prettiness of her features, the bruises from the other day already almost healed.

"Siobhan, what are you doing here?" I asked. It probably wasn't the most tactful way to put it, but I wasn't in the mood for it this morning. And she *had* broken into my office before.

"I… I came to see you." Siobhan frowned. "Are you okay, Elle?"

I was about to say yes, of course, but honestly, I'd known Siobhan longer than most of the people around me. I sat down on the edge of Fergie's desk. "No, not really."

"What's up, boss?" Fergie echoed. "More on the Jessica Hammersmith thing?"

Maybe I shouldn't have said anything. Maybe Niall deserved a chance to explain things. But at the same time, I knew if I didn't tell someone about what I'd found, I'd go mad thinking about it. I'd certainly go mad waiting to talk it over with a man who thought that distracting me with sex was the best way to handle a conversation that he would rather not have.

So, I told them. I told them about the club. I told them about Jessica going there. I told them about what I'd found in Niall's study, and about just how evasive he'd been when I'd asked him to talk to me about it all. I told them everything, until by the end of it, I just felt empty, because laying it out there for them, I already knew what they would say.

"Niall did it, didn't he?" I said.

Fergie shrugged. "There could be an innocent explanation. We've discussed a few possibilities to explore."

"Do any of them actually explain the facts, Fergie?"

"Well, maybe not all of them," Fergie admitted.

"Did you find some perfect alternative explanation for the disappearances of the other people?" I asked. "The ones the coven is so upset about?"

Fergie shook his head. "I've only just managed to compile a list of likely looking disappearances. I haven't got much more than that."

I sighed. "Do any of your explanations explain why Niall would have the letters he has? Why he keeps wandering off on 'business'?"

"Did you really expect that Niall would be squeaky clean? I mean, look at the way he lives. That house is the kind of place only a millionaire could afford."

I already knew Niall had money. Just look at his art collection.

"He works," I pointed out. "He has an assistant for it, he's that busy. He's always in the middle of this deal or that deal."

Except that I didn't really know what any of the business deals were all about.

"Yes," Fergie said. "I could probably get you the details for Sampson Holdings inside an hour if you wanted them. But did you think that he wouldn't use his powers to influence people for that?"

"That's not the same," I said. "What about the rest of it? The gifts?" I shut my eyes, remembering the things I'd found. "What are we saying? That Niall has used his powers to make people give him money?"

Fergie shrugged. Siobhan actually looked slightly impressed. But then, she made her living as a thief. Then she frowned.

"Everyone has their dark side, Elle," Fergie said. "I should know that, given what I am."

"But have you ever killed anyone?" I shot back. "Niall has. He's told me that much. He said it when I found out what he was."

"No, I haven't done that," Fergie admitted, "but think about when you found me, back after the accident."

I'd found Fergie after he'd been involved in an automobile accident on the last full moon. He'd been a snarling, injured werewolf, almost impossible to calm down in his four-legged form. It had taken a lot of empathic power to bring him down to a wagging tail and a lick on my hand.

Fergie looked at me, his topaz-colored eyes intent on mine. "What do you think would have happened if a hiker had found me, rather than you?"

I shook my head. "It still isn't the same thing. All those references to mysterious deaths he's kept. All the missing coven witches and warlocks. What if…" I could barely bring myself to say it. "What if they're all part of the same thing? What if Niall killed all of them?"

Siobhan was still scrabbling about under the table. "Um… I think we have a problem."

"Because Elle thinks her boyfriend is a mass murderer?" Fergie shot back, with plenty of sarcasm. "You don't say."

"No." Siobhan straightened up, holding something in between her thumb and forefinger. It was tiny, and obviously electronic. "I mean, we have a problem because Elle has just *said* that she thinks that, and…well, I think you've been bugged."

* Chapter Nine *

One thing I'd learned in my job: always keep a change of clothes nearby. Actually, I'd learned that one chasing after Fergie through the mud of a Highlands forest. So, I grabbed a spare skirt, blouse, and underwear out of a drawer of my desk, disappeared into the office stationary cupboard for a minute or two, and tried to work out what I was going to do while I changed.

I had to get to Niall. That much was obvious. The only people I could think of who might use bugs were the coven. If the coven had bugged us, then they knew every doubt I had. They knew all about Niall's past now, and that would just make him look even guiltier than he had before in their eyes. Maybe, *maybe* Rebecca would stall them, either out of whatever lingering friendship she had for me, or more likely out of fear of what I would do if she didn't, but how long would it be before assassins got after him, the way they'd gone after me? Would some coven gunman be lining up his sights on Niall even as I sat there?

An even harder question: should I let them?

That thought came out of nowhere, and I shoved it away on instinct, yet it came back all too easily. I was asking myself what I should do when it came to Niall, but what did that mean? If he had killed Jessica Hammersmith, what *could* I do about it? If he'd killed all these people, what was I willing to do about it? Niall said that I had the potential to be stronger than him, the way witches were almost always stronger than warlocks, yet, if I wasn't willing to do anything, did it *matter* how strong I was?

If I just left Niall to go on as he was, how long would it be before he killed again? And again. I would be as good as condemning the next Jessica Hammersmith who fell into his path. If I couldn't bring myself to stop him, then maybe the best thing I could do was to stand back and let the coven do its work.

I shook my head. *No.* I couldn't let that happen. I wouldn't let that happen. I had to at least try to talk to Niall before it came to that. Maybe I could convince him.

I came out of the cupboard looking far more businesslike than I had looked going into it. Siobhan was still holding the bug. I took it from her and held it up in front of me. I needed it.

"Is this thing still working?"

"I don't know," Siobhan said. "Maybe. Elle—"

"If you can hear me," I said into the bug, "listen to me. Whatever else you have heard, whatever he might have done, Niall is mine. *Mine.* Attack him, Rebecca, and I will come for you. If he needs to be stopped…if he needs to be stopped, I'll be the one to stop him."

I crushed the bug in a heavy-duty stapler, looking around at Fergie and Siobhan, almost daring them to say something.

"Fergie, Niall's Aston will have a GPS tracker on it in case of theft. Can you call up the location?"

"I'm not some teenaged hacking prodigy, you know," Fergie replied.

"You don't need to be," I said. "Just call the insurers and let them know that we need the location for a case."

"Lie to the people who pay us?" Fergie asked. He obviously caught sight of my expression. "All right. I'll get right on it."

I waited while he made the call.

Siobhan touched my shoulder lightly. "Are you really planning to…you know? Kill him?"

"I don't know," I admitted. "I can't let him murder people."

Siobhan bit her lip. She looked lost then, almost…terrified. I didn't have the time to spare for comforting goblins right then though.

"Elle…I don't think Niall…" Siobhan began and then her voice faded out.

"I have the GPS on screen," Fergie called out. "The car is parked close to the castle area."

"Great." I couldn't keep the disappointment out of my voice. The main tourist space of the city. One that would be thronging right now. "It's only the perfect space for him to hunt."

"And you, too," Siobhan ventured.

"Right," I said. "Wait here. If the car moves, you tell me."

Siobhan caught hold of my arm. "Elle, there's something I have to—"

"Not *now*, Siobhan," I said, brushing her off as I headed for the door. It was harsher than it needed to be, but right then, I'd been lied to and abandoned, shot at and accused. I had a boyfriend to confront and a murder to solve. I figured all of that earned me the right to be a little harsh.

It didn't take me long to get over to the castle. I rushed through the old town, past all the tourist shops and the small cafés, until I was standing beneath the ancient stone edifice on its hill, the familiar cannon that sounded their regular salute sticking out from the battlements. The crowds were already thick up Lawnmarket and Castle Hill, with clumps of tourists standing around the edges of those streets taking photographs while street performers continued to take up space as they vied for attention.

I didn't look at any of them closely. I didn't drift through the emotion the way I had yesterday, either. Instead, I scanned the crowd, looking for some sign of Niall as I made my way up the hill. I was heading for the castle only on instinct, because the truth was that Niall could be anywhere. I could have missed him a dozen times and not known it, yet some hunch kept me going. Some fragment of memory.

I opened my senses as wide as I dared, taking in the feel of the people around me, searching for some hint of that feeling that signified another like me. There, up further, heading into the castle, I felt the sharp otherness of another enchanter. It had to be Niall.

There was a line waiting to get in. I ignored it, pushing power into the men who tried to step into my path so hard that they practically fell to their knees as they let me pass. I headed up through the winding complexity of the old fortress, which had stood up to wars and the displeasure of kings, but really wouldn't want to be in the way of my current mood.

The castle. I'd been here before, once, at school, as a child. My main memory of it was of getting lost in its maze of corridors and having to call out for help. As a child, it had seemed such a huge, intimidating place. As an adult, it had seemed like the kind of place to ignore as a tourist trap, the kind of place to quietly laugh about busloads of people from south of the border coming up to see while I got to see all the "real" places in the city. As an enchantress, it looked completely different.

For a start, I could feel all the layers of history that had seeped into the stone around me. Not in the way that some of the tourists around me would probably claim to feel it. Even the ones with their own "ghost-busting" equipment were deluding themselves. Instead, I could feel layer upon layer of emotion, from the most recent blend of curiosity and impatience belonging to the tourists around me, through the pain of wars and the glory of state occasions, all the way back to the toil and effort of the castle's builders.

More importantly, I could see what a perfect hunting ground the place made for an enchantress. All those nooks and crannies dotted around gave someone like me the perfect places in which to trap a human and feed. All those areas that were marked off limits to the general public, in which a skilled hunter could lurk and draw a victim…beckoned. All those potential victims wandering around in their little groups, or better yet, trying to hang back to get the feeling of independence from their tour party. It was tempting. The dark, hungry part of me whispered just how easy it would be to send a tendril of interest over to one of them, to draw them back into a dark spot where I could feed.

I ignored my hunger, looking through the crowd, following the feeling of an enchanter until I saw…

Niall was ahead of me. There was no mistaking his bright halo of blond hair, even in the midst of the crowd. His clothes were more subdued than usual, though. A simple dark jacket and jeans seemed so out of place on him but fit so well with the rest of the crowd that he was practically invisible in it. From the way he moved carefully through the groups of people, never striding, never looking up, I guessed that was his intention. I could *feel* that was his intention, because ahead of me I could feel the steady pulse of power, encouraging people to look away. Encouraging eyes to slide right off him.

Mine might have done the same, had my other, more magical, senses not been so carefully fixed on the idea of him. I knew from experience that what Niall was doing was almost as good as being invisible. I'd used the technique myself to persuade an art gallery full of people to look away while I'd threatened Rebecca once.

There could be only one reason for Niall to do it now.

He was hunting.

I had been planning to confront Niall straight away when I found him. If I'd found him. I had been planning to walk up to him and demand answers, and this time not to accept "tomorrow" as an answer. Now, though, I found myself falling into step behind him, pushing out my own "don't notice me" signals to the crowd around me. If I followed, I could see what he was going to do. I *had* to see what he was going to do. If I saw it with my own eyes, then there could be no doubt left. There would be no more avoiding it. I would know what he was. Everything that he was.

And if I caught him in the act, I resolved that I would do what I needed to do to keep him from hurting or killing anyone else. Regardless of the way my heart protested at the thought. So, I followed without taking action yet, watching as Niall moved through the crowd, looking this way and that with occasional hurried glances. Did he know I was behind him? I didn't think so, but…

But if not, what was he doing? Picking out a target? Perhaps he was just making sure that he had a clear line of escape picked out. A spot in which to feed. If he did find a target to his liking, what then? At what point should I intervene? When he chose them? When he moved in? When he dragged them away to some hidden spot to take their energy? After that, when he was sated? How far would he feed? To the death? Would he leave behind the empty shell of some tourist? No. Surely, he would just—

Then, suddenly, I saw *her*.

Victoria was up on the battlements, looking out over the city from a spot next to the largest of the castle's cannons. She was elegantly dressed in dark pants and a cream silk t-shirt, her hair moving slightly in the breeze that high up. There were steps in front of her, but Niall stepped past them, avoiding her line of sight and moving toward a second set that was maybe a hundred yards further along.

He was stalking her, I was sure of it. It was too much of a coincidence to believe that after Jessica's death at the hands of an enchanter, Niall should just *happen* to show up at a place where her lover was taking in the sights. He'd come for her.

What he intended to do with her, I didn't know. Did he want to frighten Victoria off? To merely start the process of feeding from her? To kill her? Given what had happened to Jessica, I knew I couldn't take the risk. I had to get her to safety.

I sprinted up the steps in front of me. Unlike Niall, I didn't care if Victoria saw me or not.

"Elle?" She looked at me in obvious surprise, her hand going up to her throat.

"There's no time to explain what I'm doing here." I reached out, grabbing her arm. "You need to come with me, right now."

"But—"

"Victoria, I believe your life is in imminent danger. Come on. No, not that way. Back down the stairs."

I practically dragged her along after me, leading her down the stairs as quickly as I could. After the first few yards, her mouth opened in a question, but I shook my head.

"You're going to have to trust me," I said.

I glanced back, but there was no sign of Niall. That had to be a good thing. My best chance of getting Victoria out of there safely was if he didn't spot us. If he didn't have the opportunity to give chase. I just had to hope that the slow movement of the tour parties kept him from viewing our progress from the top of the wall for long enough. I put my arm around Victoria's waist, walking her back through the castle toward the exit, forcing her to keep moving.

"Elle, what's going on?" she demanded, about halfway there. "I mean, you say my life is in danger. Does that mean—"

"Right now, the man who killed Jessica is in this castle," I said, and as I said it, I knew it had to be true. The only reason Niall might be here stalking Victoria was if he had killed Jessica and wanted to finish the job. Maybe he'd even set it up like this, feeding on one of them, and then putting himself in a position to feed on the other.

Victoria stopped. "If you know who it is, and he's here, we shouldn't leave. We should call the police. We need to—"

"No police. You need to run. Now." I shoved her a pace or two in the direction of the exit. "Get out of here, go home, lock the doors and don't let anyone in except for me. I'll deal with things here."

"You promise?" Victoria looked at me seriously. "Promise me that the man who did this to Jess isn't getting away with it?"

I nodded. "I promise. Now run for it. Before it is too late."

She ran. I turned back toward the battlements, thinking about the promise I had just made, and how I was going to manage to keep it.

* Chapter Ten *

By the time Niall made it up there, I was sitting on the cannon. It was the kind of thing that people were explicitly banned from doing, but right then, I was pushing out a flat wall of inattention, so it wasn't like anyone was exactly going to tell me to stop. Besides, I wanted to make an impression.

I did. Niall saw me as he reached the top of the steps. I had the brief satisfaction of seeing his eyes widen in surprise that I had tailed him there. I could feel the shock coming off him, and the hurt. No, that wasn't right. *He* didn't get to be the hurt one in this situation. Not after what he'd done.

"Well, well," I said. "Come here often?"

"What are you *doing* here, Elle?" he asked as he came forward. I could feel him pushing people out as hard as I was, making our own private bubble in the middle of the crowd. People walked around us without even knowing that they were doing it, giving us a wide berth on either side.

"What am I doing here?" I shook my head. "Perhaps I should be asking what *you* are doing here, Niall?"

He hesitated, and I could feel the conflicting emotions coming out of him in a tangle too complicated to unpick.

"Don't even think about holding something back from me," I snapped. I'd had enough. I stepped forward, jabbing him in his chest with a finger. "I am sick of your secrets."

"If I have kept secrets," Niall insisted, "it was for your own protection. There are things that I was worried about telling you, things that might have made our relationship too complicated. And things that would have hurt you more than I could stand."

"Like what?" I demanded. "Like you being a murderer?"

"A what? Elle, are you mad? Do you really believe that I would do something like that?"

"What else can I think?"

I could feel the fury rising in him as his back stiffened and he shifted into something that wasn't quite a defensive stance. Like he thought I might attack him there and then. Or maybe the point was that the words were enough of an attack. Niall froze, staring at me. His expression was cold, but I could feel the heat of his anger beneath it all too easily.

Not that being able to feel his emotions had helped me before. It should have meant that we had no secrets from one another, but time and again, he'd shown me that it didn't work like that.

"You think I would lie to you?" Niall asked.

I laughed. "Yes. Yes, Niall, I think you would lie to me. Constantly. Totally. When we first met, you completely deceived me. You tricked me about what you were. You lied to me about your 'stolen' painting."

"You know why I did all that. I wanted to meet you. I couldn't just walk up to you and introduce myself on the street. You would have run. If not from me, then from what you were." He paused. "You truly believe that I killed this woman whose death you are investigating?"

"Jessica. Her name was Jessica Hammersmith. After everything you've done, at least have the courtesy to use it." His anger might be bubbling up under the surface, but right then, mine was blazing hotter. He wasn't going to get to deny his involvement in this.

"That's what you think? After everything I have done? After how close we have gotten? You can believe this?"

"Do you think I *like* feeling like this?" I demanded.

Niall shook his head. "I did not kill this woman."

"You can't even say her name."

"I didn't kill Jessica Hammersmith."

"It's too late to try lying. You killed her. What I want to hear now is why."

"You're wrong," he said flatly.

I took a step back from him. "You think I can't feel an enchanter around a murder scene? You think that you get to deny it when your traces are all over this? Am I meant to believe that you would never kill?"

"Yes."

"You've told me that you've killed people. I *saw* you kill Evert. What is to stop you from killing them now?"

Niall stood very still, his hands balled into fists with the tension. "The warlock was self-defense. As for the others… that was a long time ago. The circumstances were different."

"Fine. How about if we discuss the circumstances?" I ventured. "You didn't tell me that you spent your life tricking people out of their money. What was it? You'd find some rich woman, get her to bankroll you, and then slowly drain her? I've looked in the box, Niall."

"What box?"

"The trinket box in your office."

"You had no *right*." That made his anger flash all the way to his eyes. Not the thought of being caught. Not the thought that someone had died. Just that I had touched his stupid box.

"You left me with no choice," I said. "You wouldn't tell me anything, so I had to look for myself."

"You had no right to look in that box," Niall insisted again. "The things in there…they are too personal."

"What was I supposed to do?" I demanded. "A woman is dead. Do you even care?"

"Of course I care. She's a human being. A life lost."

"For someone who claims to care, you don't seem all that upset." I could hear how much I'd raised my voice by that point, but it didn't matter. The strangest part was the way people just kept walking past us in our little bubble of isolation. It was as if no one could see us or hear us. We could probably have had a full-scale battle and no one would have noticed except for the two of us. Maybe we were going to, given the way things were heading.

"What am I meant to do?" I asked, and I couldn't keep the sadness out of my voice.

"You're supposed to trust me," Niall said.

"Trust you? How on Earth could I trust you when you won't tell me anything?" I stood there, my hands on my hips. "I've spent the past few weeks practically living with you, and yet I still feel like I hardly know anything about you outside of the bedroom at night. When I wake up, you're gone. I wake up alone and every time I feel like you stole something from me."

"I have never taken anything from you," Niall insisted. "You know that our kind cannot take energy from one another. We can only give."

"I'm not *talking* about energy," I snapped back. "I'm talking about trust. I'm talking about love. I give you that, and you're never there."

Somehow, this had become about more than the murder. How? Maybe because I knew this would be the only opportunity to have this argument.

"I know every inch of your body," I said, "and I still don't know you. I don't even know why you're gone every morning."

"Don't you?" Niall demanded. "Or is it just that you don't *let* yourself know?"

I stepped back until my back was against the cannon again. "What's that supposed to mean?"

"I go out to feed. I have ever since we met. I have told you, it is what we are. Yet, you have been so determined to ignore it that you haven't even asked."

"There have been plenty of things I *have* asked," I countered. "I don't remember getting answers to those either. I don't know where you were born, what you've spent your life doing, Anything."

"Because none of that matters," Niall insisted. "That was then. This is now. We matter, but the past does not. I live in the present, with you. The things in that box...they are reminders of the past for me. Not for anyone else. Not even for you. Why can't you see that? Things in there...I never wanted you to see those things."

"I'll bet you didn't." I took a breath. "Tell me, Niall, what about the witches and warlocks who are missing? Do you know how hard it has been to keep the coven from coming after you for that?"

"So, you have been talking to the coven about me."

I reached out to touch the cannon. Somehow, there was something stable about the feel of something so solid under my fingers. "Anyone *else* would have killed you by now."

"And is that what you intend to do?" Niall asked. He didn't raise his voice. He just stood there, staring at me, waiting for an answer. "*Could* you?"

"Tell me about the box," I insisted, ignoring the question. Mostly because even now, when it was clear what he'd done, I didn't have an answer.

"No." Niall shook his head. "The past is the past. My past is done with. It isn't coming back. I will *not* go back there. Not even for you."

"You aren't exactly making this simple." I stepped around almost to the other side of the cannon. I didn't want to give him an easy escape route.

"I *am* making this simple," Niall pointed out. "Not easy, perhaps, but simple. You believe me or you don't. You love me or you don't."

"You aren't going to give an inch, are you?" I demanded. "After everything I've given up for you. The coven. My life. My friends."

Niall looked indignant this time. "You didn't give up *anything*. You still try to live your life as if you are some protected little witch. You will not even bend enough to feed, because the thought disgusts you. I have given you everything I am. Everything I am *now*. What I *was* should not matter. I cannot change the past. I have stayed in this city for you, even though the threat—"

"The threat from the coven wouldn't even exist if you hadn't started playing games!"

"Games? What games?"

"With them. With me!" I was shouting now, really shouting. "I've gone to so much trouble protecting you. I even threatened the coven for you. I threatened Rebecca when this started. When she thought you were going after her people. But they were right. You're nothing but a killer!"

"I did not kill Jessica Hammersmith," Niall said, evenly. "And I have done nothing to those witches and warlocks of this city who have not come after me."

Somehow, that attempt at reasonableness just made me angrier. "And you expect me to believe that's true just because you say it is?"

"Yes. You say that you love me, but you haven't trusted me once. Not about anything that matters."

It wasn't enough. Not anymore. I shook my head. "It doesn't work like that. I mean, do you even deny that you're here…hunting?"

Niall paused again, and again, it told me everything I needed to know. He made a hurt noise in his throat.

"Come on," I insisted. "Say it. You were here hunting."

"Of course I was hunting," Niall shot back. He wasn't anywhere near as controlled as usual. "And you manage to make even *that* sound dirty, as though it is something that our kind should not do. As if it is not a natural part of our existence."

I'd expected all kinds of things from Niall when I confronted him. Anger, guilt, confession… everything except indignation. "We—"

"We are *predators*!" Niall's voice had risen to match my own inside our little bubble of silence. I hadn't seen this side of him before. "We hunt. We take life force from humans. We can no more stop hunting than a human can choose to stop breathing. It is what we do. It is what we *are*."

I shook my head. "It isn't what I am."

"No," Niall snapped back, "because you would rather pretend to be something else. You deny you are a predator, yet you would bleed my staff dry with your pretending. You treat your hunger as if it is something to be afraid of."

"It *is* something to be afraid of," I said. I could still remember the night when Niall had first told me what I was. I had almost drained his assistant Marie, simply because the hunger had been too much. I had ended up knocking her down and running. "If I don't control it, people will get hurt."

"You are not controlling it," Niall insisted. "Not truly."

I shook my head. "No. I control it now. I don't let the hunger control me."

"By draining my staff, piece by piece? You leave them exhausted, and you give nothing back."

I cringed. "I'm not hurting them."

"You're using them, and that *is* hurting them. My housekeeper, Kelly, is exhausted. My driver, David, falls asleep at the wheel. Even me. You would rather have me feed you scraps of emotion secondhand to keep your conscience clean than admit what you are."

"It isn't about that," I insisted. How had this conversation gotten twisted around to me?

"Isn't it? One taste from a human the right way, and you turned away in disgust."

He meant the bartender I'd kissed, obviously. I thought we'd dealt with that. Except we hadn't dealt with it, had we? We'd just brushed it aside.

"You don't dictate how I feed," I said.

"I can tell you one thing, Elle. I cannot feed you anymore. I will not. You are perfectly capable of feeding yourself now. Of course, that will mean going out and hunting for yourself, but maybe I have been too lenient in the way I have taught you."

"Lenient?" I bristled while the crowd swirled around us on the battlements. "I'm not your student."

"No? Go out and get your own sustenance, and then tell me that you know everything. You want to be an enchantress? I had to learn what I was in far harsher ways. I did not get the *choice* of feeding so delicately, and yet you want to attack me for being what I am."

"A killer."

"You were born to this, just like me."

Just like that, I could feel something shatter between us. I had known that coming after him like this had its risks, yet even so, the reality of this moment, just feeling that dead weight as I knew that things couldn't be right again between us, was too much.

"So," I said, and now my voice was quiet, "where does this leave us?"

"That is up to you. It was always up to you." Niall stepped back from me. "If you truly believe that I killed this woman, after all I have said…well, you must treat me as a murderer." Niall spread his hands.

He still wanted me to believe that he hadn't done it, yet how could I? There had been an enchanter in Jessica Hammersmith's house. That wasn't something someone could fake, not to me. She had hanged herself, and only an enchanter would have been able to make her feel the driven despair that led to it. Niall had openly admitted that he had been hunting. Then there were all the other people who were missing.

All of the pieces to the puzzle were there, but I still wanted to hear him say it, if only to put off the moment when I would have to work out what I was going to do. With the emotion of a castle full of tourists around me, I could draw emotion from them and convert it into enough energy to throw almost any spell I wanted. I could envelop Niall in flames or blast him with force. I could treat him exactly as a murderer. I could kill him in a dozen different ways, but any one of them would feel like I'd be killing a part of myself. Yet, what else could I do?

"Say it, Niall," I said. "*Say it.* You killed Jessica. You came here to kill Victoria."

"Victoria?" Niall's eyes widened slightly. "You know about Victoria?"

"Of course I know about Victoria. She's Jessica's lover, and you came here to finish what you started."

"No, Elle, you don't understand—"

Niall didn't finish that sentence, because in that moment I felt something I had felt before, on the way back from Arthur's Seat. The laser-like focus of someone staring down the sight of a gun. Having been shot at once, it wasn't a feeling I was ever going to forget.

"Niall! Look out!"

I threw myself flat on the ground as the first shot skittered off the crenulations. Niall did the same. What sort of idiot shot at people standing in a castle? Particularly one where there were still soldiers garrisoned, more than capable of shooting back, even if the majority of people still thought of it as a tourist attraction?

I huddled in behind the cannon, using the bulk of it as a barrier. Niall did the same.

"Who is shooting?" Niall asked me, and I realized that I could hear him normally. As opposed, for example, to being in the middle of a screaming crowd of terrified tourists. Apparently, our efforts to avoid being seen extended even to being shot at. It was a surreal situation, sitting there, frightened for my life, while just below a tour guide continued to talk about James VI and I.

"Probably the coven," I snapped back at him. "It's happened before."

"What? When? And you didn't *tell* me?"

"You do *not* get to play that card. Not now."

"You didn't tell me that something like this had happened? Elle! Please…"

"Stay down! They aren't done yet." I could still feel that narrow flicker of concentration moving over the battlements around us. The moment one of us moved, we would be a target. "This would be a really good moment to tell me that an enchantress' powers include an immunity to bullets that I don't know about."

Niall didn't have an answer for that and for the first time, I felt a tendril fear emanating from him.

"No," he said, "we aren't invulnerable. We can heal quickly, if we have the energy. We can be faster and stronger than humans. A bullet that does enough damage, though…"

I understood. Even with all the power at our disposal, we could be dead before we had a chance to recover.

"There," Niall said. "More of them."

I looked where Niall was looking. A quartet of people was pushing its way through the crowd, against the general flow. I recognized Rebecca at their head. There were two women and a man with her, or rather, two witches and a warlock.

"Battle witches, probably," Niall said, with a glance down at them. "A coven hit squad."

It made sense. The shooter had to be with them. After all, who else could it be? This was Scotland, not the Wild West.

"Will this never be over with the coven, Elle?"

"I tried to make peace," I pointed out. "I tried, and then *someone* had to go around attacking people."

"I have already told you—"

"Forget it, Niall," I said. Rebecca and the others were blocking the closest exit, straight down the nearest stairs. There were the ones further back, from which we could have disappeared into the corridors and twists of the castle, but standing to reach them would have exposed us to the sniper. We needed another option. A distraction.

I felt the cold iron of the old cannon beneath my hands, and I suddenly knew what I needed to do. Of course, if I did it, Niall had as much of a chance to run as I did. I didn't care right then. I might not know what *I* was going to do when it came to Niall, but I knew that the coven *certainly* wasn't getting to kill him.

"Get ready to run down the far stairs," I shouted to Niall, simultaneously stopping my distraction for the crowd. "We can sneak down through the castle."

I pulled in energy from the people around us as fast as I could, trying to shape it, but mostly just forcing the magic down into the cannon until…

The cannon went off, but just saying that wasn't sufficient to cover the sheer power of it so close. With the magic running through it, what came out wasn't the simple boom of a blank round. Instead, color and power burst out, exploding above the city streets. The recoil from it was enough to blast Niall and me from our feet.

As we scrambled to get our arms and legs untangled, the tourists yelled as they saw what came out of the mouth of the cannon and shot into the sky above us. The tourists were used to smaller cannon blasts to mark the hours, but this was on another scale. A whole fireworks display compressed into one roaring burst from the beast of a cannon that we had hidden behind. Everyone in the castle stared up at it, and about half of them started to applaud the unexpected entertainment. The other half were just yelling.

My ears were ringing from the boom, but I turned to Niall.

"Run! Now!" I yelled, sprinting for the stairs.

I stopped when I saw that he wasn't following.

Instead, he'd gone the other way and I felt the invisible thread stretching and breaking as he went away from me. I cried out, shocked to see him heading straight toward Rebecca and the other witches. Instead of running from them, he moved forward like the predator he was, obviously ready for battle. It seemed insane. Physically, even Niall shouldn't have been able to stand up to four trained combat witches at once.

It was only then that I realized that he didn't plan on this being physical. I felt him twisting the emotions of the crowd as he went. And not in a good way.

"No! Niall, *don't!*"

My protest came too late. I could feel the ugliness of the crowd's emotions as Niall altered them, taking the feelings of ordinary, pleasant people and pouring anger into them until it overflowed. So much anger that it was hard to see where he could have gotten it all from. Was that really how he felt?

I didn't have enough time to focus on that though, because I was too busy watching as Niall transformed the crowd below into something closer to a mob. A mob that he focused, shaping their anger, directing it at his enemies. I could see the crush of angry tourists as they started toward Rebecca and her cronies, their eyes narrowed with malicious intent and their fists ready. Old, young, it didn't matter. Grandmothers, students, mothers with toddlers, foreign tourists with too many cameras, they all came forward in a rush.

Rebecca knocked one of them back with a push of force, but there was only so much she could do while still being subtle. Hands grabbed for her, pulling at her, shoving her. I saw a big man in work clothes throw a wide, swinging punch at the warlock.

Amazingly, it connected. More than that, it connected hard enough that the warlock went down before he even had a chance to use his magic. What kind of combat-trained warlock couldn't block a punch? Immediately, someone else threw a kick and he yelped.

Briefly, I thought about leaving Rebecca and her people to their fate at the hands of the crowd. I had warned the coven about what might happen if they came after us. I had warned and warned them, holding back even when they attacked us. Even so, I knew I couldn't live with myself if I walked away now. I couldn't leave them. Not if I wanted to go on living in Edinburgh. Not if I wanted to be able to live with myself.

So, I rushed down there, reaching for the same emotions Niall had used, trying to untangle what he had tangled up. It was nearly impossible to do anything cleanly, especially with so many people around me, jostling and pushing as I tried to force my way through them. Niall had decades more experience than I did. So I didn't try to do it cleanly. I just did what I had to do. I got in there like it was a mosh pit at a club and I sucked the emotion out of the air.

I took all the emotion I could take, dragging in the hatred and the anger of the mob, swallowing it down and trying to transmute it as it went. I couldn't permanently hold the emotions of a crowd. They would snap back to their owners like elastic. I couldn't feed off them, I couldn't take away the anger, but I *could* hold all that bile and resentment Niall had thrown in for a few seconds at least, giving people a chance to look around and wonder what they were doing.

People stopped in the middle of assaulting Rebecca's witches, looking around, bewildered and half-ashamed.

I breathed out, and with it, I breathed out calm, peace, and love. As much of it as I could manage without emptying myself completely. I took the energy of the anger, changing it, soothing it as I breathed that energy back out.

It wasn't as skillful or subtle as Niall's manipulation, but I knew I had the advantage when it came to the sheer power I could handle. I twisted back what he had twisted, not through skill but through simple volume of effort, pouring out calm until it didn't feel like there was anything left in me. It was like exhaling a breath, then keeping going far beyond my lungs' capacity.

Even so, it took time to do it. A mob has its own momentum, and by the time I had defused this one, Rebecca's team didn't look too good. The warlock on the ground was bruised and bloodied—he was breathing but unconscious. One of the women had what looked like a broken arm. None of them was uninjured. This close, they didn't look much like members of a crack assassination team anymore, either. They all looked too frightened, too injured. Too ordinary. Between the four of them, they should have been able to deal with the crowd far better, if they had been trained.

Rebecca was the least hurt of all of them. When she saw me looking back at her, she flinched but did not run.

"This is the second time you've come after Niall and me," I said, walking right up to her.

She grimaced and swallowed hard. She started to say something, but I didn't give her a chance. Instead, I lashed out with a wave of emotion that sent her reeling back against her friends. Any more, and it might have sent her mad. I didn't care. I wanted her to know that there would be a reckoning.

Then I set off after Niall, hoping that I could catch up with him before he disappeared into the city crowds. Most of all, I hoped that I could catch him before he hurt anyone else.

* Chapter Eleven *

Niall was truly gone by the time I got back out onto Castle Hill, the traces of him lost in the sea of human emotions all around me. That, or I simply couldn't bring myself to look for him as hard as I had on the way to the castle. I didn't want to fight him. I certainly didn't want to kill him. Yet, with everything he had done, what else was there for me to do?

Maybe I could force him to go away. To go far, far away and never come back. To go somewhere on the other side of the world, where I wouldn't have to worry about what he was doing. Where I wouldn't have to think about him.

It was a coward's way out, because it wouldn't do anything to stop him killing there, yet even the thought of that hurt like someone was ripping my heart from my chest. I told it to stop, that exile was better than the alternative, and it made no difference. My heart was breaking. My lover was a murderer. How had I got to this point? How had I let things get this far? Would it have been easier if I had just let Rebecca and Evert kill him when I first found out what he was?

No, because then I would never have found out what *I* was. Although maybe my life would have been simpler that way too. I didn't have the time to think about that now though. It was far too late for regrets. Now, I just needed to stop Niall from killing again.

First, I needed to find Niall. I didn't waste time trying to scour the streets for him. I'd missed that chance. Instead, I headed right for his house, knowing that he would need to go back there. There was too much there for him to leave it behind. I latched onto the emotions of the crowd around me, using them to fuel a sprint across the city that I wouldn't have thought possible until I did it.

Which meant that barely ten minutes later, I hammered on Niall's front door hard enough that it splintered the wood. Marie opened the door and I shoved her out of the way, roughly enough that she stumbled.

"Where is he?"

"Elle, what are you doing? What's wrong?"

"Where is he?" I demanded, and this time, I put every ounce of anger I could into it. Niall's assistant quailed back, and there was a part of me that liked that, that said I should take that fear and swallow it, that I should feed and not stop feeding until there was nothing left of her but an empty husk.

"Elle, please. Niall isn't even here." I could feel the panic rising behind the words. Of course, Marie had been here before. She knew about this side of me. Had she known about that side of Niall, too? The only reason I didn't pounce on her then was that it would make me no better than Niall was.

Besides, I could feel for myself that she was telling the truth. I would know if Niall were there in the house. Even so, I plunged deeper into the building, throwing open doors and moving through the rooms, wanting to make sure, looking for… I didn't know what.

"Where did he go?" I asked as Marie followed me.

"I don't know. What is this all about?"

I continued my path through the house, throwing open doors as I went.

"Elle, what are you doing? You can't just—"

"Marie, I'm investigating a murder, and if I were you, I'd stay away from me right now." I didn't even have to use my power on her. She ran off, slamming the door to her office behind her. I heard it lock, for all the good that would do if I really wanted to get in. I could tear the lock away easily if I needed.

Right then, I had other concerns.

"Niall!" I yelled and my own voice echoed back at me in the long hallway.

Why was I doing this? Why was I storming through the house so blindly? I didn't know. Maybe I was hoping that I could find a clue as to where he might have gone? Maybe I was just looking for all those things that would show me I should have known he was a murderer all along. Maybe I didn't know what I wanted.

Whatever the reason, I ended up in Niall's art gallery. There weren't as many pieces as there had been in there, thanks to the long-term loans I'd convinced him to make to the City Art Centre, but there were still a few. Modern sculptures on plinths, a few paintings. I had to fight the urge to pick up things and start smashing them, one by one, to feed something to my anger. The reason I didn't was because I couldn't do that to the art, not because I couldn't do that to Niall.

Suddenly, I stopped in my tracks, my heart overruling my head. I stared at the plinth where we had first made love all those weeks ago, unable to even think as I stood there. I picked up the sculpture on it and I threw it, watching it splinter against the wall, tracing the arcs of the fragments. I still just felt… empty. I slumped against the plinth and sank to the floor, sitting there, waiting, my hopes as shattered as the pottery.

A lump rose in my throat as I tried to work out how I had been so stupid. As I tried to work out what I would say when Niall showed up. Niall would be back. He had to be. He wouldn't abandon all this, would he? He wouldn't abandon *me*, would he?

Yet, what if he did? What if he walked away without looking back? I'd been thinking of telling him to leave the city, but that felt so different than the idea of him just running away without even saying goodbye.

That was why I waited. I waited there for an hour or more, even after it became obvious that Niall wasn't coming back to his home. I waited even though my phone was going off as people tried to get through to me, ignoring them on the basis that none of the callers was Niall. I waited even though a part of me knew he could be on a plane by now, leaving the country, leaving me.

That, or maybe the coven had gotten to him while I'd been sitting there, contemplating the tragedy that was my love life. Maybe he didn't come because he couldn't. Either way, I sat there. I was too shaken to even cry. Too stunned to know what the next step was. Niall had changed my life around completely. I'd assumed he would always be there, and now he wasn't.

I waited until Marie came in with both Fergie and Siobhan following her. It wasn't until I looked up at them through a blurred haze that I realized I had been crying.

"What are you doing here?" I asked them.

"Marie called me," Fergie said. "She said that you'd broken down the door, pushed her, and barged in here looking for Niall. She said you were furious and you didn't look like you were leaving anytime soon. She was scared of you. Frankly, Elle…what the hell is going on?"

I looked at Marie, her face tear-streaked with mascara. Somehow, I kept doing this to her. "I'm sorry, Marie."

"If I understood, I might forgive you." Marie paused after she said it, obviously expecting an explanation.

I sighed. "It's kind of complicated. I'm sorry I lashed out. It…it's Niall."

"Did you *find* Niall?" Fergie asked. There was a carefully neutral note in his voice. He obviously wanted to help, but I could tell he didn't like that I'd nearly attacked Marie again. What did I expect, given how much he clearly liked her?

I swallowed. "I found him earlier. He did it, Fergie. He actually did it."

Fergie looked down at me in surprise and gave me a hand to help me up off the floor. "He confessed?"

"He didn't have to. He was stalking Jessica's girlfriend, and when I confronted him…"

"But he didn't confess outright?" Fergie waved Siobhan forward. The young goblin looked pretty nervous about it—her eyes barely darted to the valuable artwork all around her—but she stepped forward. "Siobhan has something she needs to tell you."

"Can't it wait?" I demanded, standing taller now that I was off the floor.

Fergie shook his head. "You need to hear her out. I tried calling you, but you didn't answer your phone."

I was probably a little busy being shot at. That or watching my lover stalk someone. Even so, Fergie seemed to think that it was important, and while I might not trust the lawyer to be my backup in a fight, I knew he wouldn't tell me to listen unless it was important.

"All right," I said. I looked over at Siobhan. I couldn't have looked very comforting, because the goblin shrank back slightly. "What is it?"

"I—I tried to tell you before, back at your office, but—"

"Just tell me," I snapped, and had to stop myself from letting my anger slip any further. I tried to project an air of calm that I didn't feel, not right then. "Come on, Siobhan. You can tell me anything."

Siobhan still hesitated for a second. "There's…there's another enchantress."

"What?" I'd grabbed Siobhan before I even realized what I was doing, half-lifting her off her feet by the collar of her hooded top.

"Another enchantress is in the city," Siobhan managed. "Please, I tried to tell you."

"Not very hard, you didn't." I shook her. "And what about when we met at Arthur's Seat? You told me that it was just me and Niall. I asked you outright if there were any others like us, and you said no. You lied."

"Stop this, Elle. She's just a girl." Fergie went to pull me away from Siobhan. It was a mistake. After everything that had happened to me today, it was about the worst mistake he could make. I threw a small fragment of what I was feeling into him and it was enough to bring him to a halt, fighting to keep from transforming under the stress.

"You lied to me," I repeated to Siobhan. "The one time it really mattered, and you lied to me. You risked my life and Niall's life. *You let me think he was a killer.*"

I didn't know what I was going to do in that moment. I could feel all the emotion in the room. I could always feel it, of course, but now it jumped and thrummed through me, as tight as a guitar string. All the fear. All the anger. All the resentment. I could feel the flickers of something more between Fergie and Marie, even while Fergie knelt there, struggling not to change.

I could feel Siobhan's guilt eating at her belly. I could feel how scared she was of me and how much she wished that she had done the right thing earlier. Right then, I wanted to eat all of it. Days of running around the city full of anxiety and suspicion had left me starving. Thinking Niall was a murderer and now this had left me on a knife-edge. In that moment, a part of me wanted to swallow all of the emotion in the room and be done with it.

"Please don't be angry," Siobhan begged. "I couldn't tell you. I *couldn't.* They would have hurt Dougie."

"Dougie? What does *this* have to do with Dougie?" I was furious that she had held back information from me. Furious enough that I didn't want to hold back anymore. Siobhan had used up her chances.

She cried out in fear and that small sound stopped me, just for a moment. I wasn't even sure why it should, when the rest hadn't. Somehow though, it was enough to make me take a look around. Fergie was down on his knees, struggling for control. Siobhan shrank away from me as far as my grip would let her, terrified that I was going to kill her for lying. Marie was caught between the need to run from me and the need to go to Fergie. What was I doing? Why was I doing this to people I really cared about?

I knew why. Niall. The hurt of losing him. I wasn't on a knife's edge. I had stepped over it, and now I had to find a way to step back. I fought for control. I took the part of me that ached to swallow the emotions around me and I made it swallow my own anger. My own grief at what I'd done. I *made* myself step back from the edge, inch by hard fought inch.

I let go of Siobhan, turning to Fergie and pumping some of the last of my waning stock of energy into calming him down. Into giving him the kind of control that I barely had. Then I looked back to my goblin friend.

"Those bruises on your face the other day…"

Siobhan swallowed. "They were from the others, not from Dougie. They hit me when I told them that you'd been nice to me and that I couldn't do this. When I said that I wouldn't trick you. That you were my friend. She watched them. She said I deserved it. I…I did deserve it."

I could feel the tangle of emotions coming up in Siobhan as she said that. She believed it, but she didn't know why. She'd been made to believe it.

"She? This enchantress you didn't tell me about?"

Siobhan nodded. "She made it seem… okay to keep her a secret from you. To do what she said."

I didn't shout now. If an enchantress had really asked her to do it…well, I knew that I could probably get Siobhan to do just about anything, if I tried hard enough. That thought took me another step back from my anger.

"I didn't know," Siobhan said. "I'm sorry. I had to. I have to. They still have Dougie. They said that if I did the wrong thing…*said* the wrong thing…they would…"

I could guess that part. "I understand, Siobhan. I'm sorry."

"I wanted to tell you from the start. I tried to explain things to her. She told me that it was all right, and then…they hurt Dougie."

Silvery tears sprang to Siobhan's eyes, but she didn't shed them. "And now, I've told you. If he dies, it's my fault."

Siobhan loved him. I knew that without having to ask. She loved him blindly, completely. Despite everything, despite the fact that I didn't even like Dougie that much, I could understand that. I knew what it was like to love someone the rest of the world hated, even past the point where it seemed to make sense.

"No. It is not your fault," I said. "But now, the only way to help Dougie is to give me as much information as possible. You need to tell me everything, Siobhan."

She nodded and the tears spilled silently.

My anger almost completely deflated as I saw that. "Tell me about this other enchantress."

"She's been living down Underneath with us for a long time," Siobhan said. "They say she used to live on the surface, but now, she prefers it with us. There are lots of us who…I guess they follow her. Treat her like she's special. She's kind of a leader. She makes it feel like…like it doesn't matter that we're trapped down there."

Well, yes. An enchantress would have an easy enough time doing that. If she wanted, I had no doubt that an enchantress could have the goblins eating out of her hand. Although why she would want to enchant goblins when she could do the same thing with humans above ground was another question.

Right then though, it didn't matter. All that mattered was the feeling of one link in the chain of logic that had condemned Niall coming undone. Jessica Hammersmith had been killed by someone like me. I'd been so sure that had to be Niall. Now…

"So, Niall is innocent?" Fergie said.

"No," I said. It still didn't work. "Maybe before he showed up at the castle, but not now. There's still too much evidence."

"Evidence can be manipulated," Fergie pointed out. "Maybe the coven? We know they bugged us and shot at you."

But there were things that didn't fit, too. The bug. Rebecca's team at the castle. Oh, I could believe that she would send a team like that. After all, she had spent my adult life watching me for the coven, ready to kill me if I showed signs of my powers, yet something about it wasn't quite right.

That kill team of Rebecca's at the castle…it just hadn't been good enough. It hadn't been the kind of thing that spoke of preparation and planning. It felt more like a group thrown together at the last minute, in an emergency. And the bug…the bug was just a little too convenient.

"It doesn't fit," I said. "Besides, none of this accounts for the presence of this enchantress. It just doesn't feel right, either."

It didn't. I wasn't quite sure why. I sat down again, trying to place it. Something about this whole business, from Jessica's death on, felt familiar. It felt like I'd lived through it before. Everyone stared at me expectantly.

"What does the enchantress look like?" I asked Siobhan.

"Well, she's beautiful," Siobhan said, but that wasn't exactly helpful. I suspected that every enchantress in the world was going to be beautiful.

"Hair? Eyes?" I asked. "Describe her for me, Siobhan. As much detail as you can remember."

Siobhan waved her hands vaguely, as though having trouble pinning down the memory. Could an enchantress do that? Could I do anything to help against it? I didn't really have the strength to push clarity into Siobhan, but I tried.

"She has dark hair, and these really deep blue eyes. I mean, when she looks at you, it's like you can't see past them. You know what I mean?"

"I know." And I did. Damn it. I stood and headed through the house, with Marie, Fergie, and Siobhan all trailing after me.

“Where are you going, Elle?” Fergie demanded.

“To prove to myself how little I pay attention sometimes.” I headed for Niall’s study. “I *saw* her. I saw her but I didn’t pay attention because I was too angry.”

Niall’s box was right where I’d left it. After all the energy I’d used recently I wasn’t sure I had the strength left for an unlocking spell so I lifted it to break it, then thought better of it. I handed it to Siobhan instead.

“Open this for me, please.”

“You can’t,” Marie said. “Niall left very *specific* instructions about never touching his box.”

“I’ve already done it once, and this time I have to, Marie.” I nodded my permission at Siobhan.

Siobhan didn’t even ask why. One good thing about having a goblin thief for an acquaintance was this: in less than a minute, I was holding an open box, rooting through it until I came up with the sepia-darkened picture of Niall and a woman I’d seen in there before. I stared at it, and now that I knew who I was looking at—it was obvious. The hat obscured her features a little, but there was really no mistaking her.

“Is this is the enchantress?” I asked Siobhan, showing her the picture. She hesitated, and then, she nodded.

“This is Victoria de Newe,” I said. “Jessica Hammersmith’s lover.”

Marie started, and I looked over at her. “Do you know that name, Marie?”

“I need to find something. There was something…” She walked out of the room.

Fergie looked longingly after her, but stayed in the room. “So, Victoria is Jessica Hammersmith’s killer?”

"Yes." It made sense now. If I had just paid more attention when I had been going through Niall's things the first time, I would even have seen it.

Fergie stared at me blankly. "I don't get it. Why would this Victoria do something like that?"

Why indeed? She hadn't drained Jessica of energy. She had destroyed her. She had poured despair into her and driven her to suicide. She had even reported it to the insurers as suspicious.

"Maybe she wanted to frame Niall for the murder and collect the insurance money?" Siobhan piped up.

I nodded. "Maybe. It's obvious that she has some connection to Niall, but the insurance money…she actually *told* me that she doesn't get it all. You checked that, Fergie, remember? Jessica's sister gets it."

"Almost all of it," Fergie agreed. "Would the remaining portion be worth killing for?"

Not on its own. There was still too much about this that I didn't understand.

Marie came back in the room, carrying a box with the coven logo on it. I'd seen it enough times back when I'd worked for them. She took a deep breath and handed it to me.

"The coven sent this?" I asked.

"I don't really know who sent it. All I know is, someone left it on the doorstep and after Niall broke the seal, he was upset. He threw it across the room. Niall never does that."

"When was this?" I asked.

"Just before all this started."

When Niall had started disappearing for meetings I didn't know about, in other words.

I opened the box and saw an aged piece of faded red ribbon inside, with knots tied in it and the ribbon cut. There was a piece of paper with it, saying simply: *Niall and Victoria*.

"What is this?" I asked.

"It's a handfasting ribbon," Marie explained.

I'd heard about the tradition. It used to be the case in Scotland that people could have a kind of 'trial marriage' for a year by being handfasted in the old way. I stared at the ribbon, letting the implications of that sink in. No wonder Niall had been so reluctant to talk about Victoria. No wonder he had been so secretive lately. And of course, it gave Victoria at least one reason to want to hurt Niall.

Except that it still didn't explain everything. It didn't explain the timing, for one thing. Why now, when Siobhan had said that Victoria had been down in the tunnels beneath the city for years? What had changed? I knew the answer to that. I knew it as soon as I asked the question. *I* had changed.

I'd known this had felt familiar, but it couldn't be that, could it? Yet, what else could it be? Which meant…

"Siobhan," I said, "I think if we find Victoria, we will find Niall. Can you show me the way into the tunnels where your people live?"

"I don't think that's a good idea," she said. "I mean, they don't really like visitors down there."

"They'll just have to learn to be more hospitable."

"We'll be lucky if they don't kill us," Siobhan said. "And what about Dougie? If I take you there, and they see you, then what will they do to him?"

I shook my head. It was a fair question. "The truth is, I don't know, Siobhan. I do know that if we don't go in there, Niall is probably in a lot of danger. Honestly, I don't think they'll exactly hold back once they don't need Dougie anymore, either. I *could* be wrong. I *could* be putting him in danger."

I paused before going on. “I think we need to get them both out of there. I think that they’ll be in more danger if we don’t go, but I’m not going to make you do this. It’s your choice.”

Siobhan was silent for several seconds, and I knew she was weighing the options. Trying to weigh the chances of getting Dougie killed against the ones of getting him back. Weighing what she owed me against the danger of getting caught. I could have pushed her then. I could have made her do what I needed her to do in order to save Niall, but I was serious about it being her choice. She’d already been manipulated too much by one enchantress, from the sounds of it.

Eventually, she nodded. “All right.”

“You’re sure Niall is even down there?” Marie asked.

I shrugged. “He wouldn’t just leave, and he isn’t here. He’s got to be Underneath.”

“Can you even hope to sneak into the goblins’ home?” Fergie asked.

I sighed and nodded at Siobhan. “Siobhan will find me a way in. As for any goblin who tries to stop me…”

“There are a *lot* of goblins down there,” Fergie said.

I shrugged, tossed the handfasting ribbon back in the box, and shoved it in my handbag. Something told me that I would need it soon enough.

“I’m coming, too,” Fergie said. “You need help.”

“Help, maybe,” I said. “Legal advice, not so much.”

“That’s low.”

I smiled. “It’s true though. Fergie, you’re a good guy. That’s kind of the problem. I might need to do things down there that won’t be good, if I want us to survive.”

Fergie started to speak again, but I held up a hand to cut him off.

"Don't get me wrong. You've helped a lot. The thing with the coven was pretty impressive, but it still doesn't make you some kind of werewolf super-warrior. Fights are about instincts as much as anything, and if it comes to one, let's face it, your first instinct is to sue."

"I can fight," Fergie insisted.

"And I can fight better. Stay here with Marie and protect her. *That's* your job right now."

"While it's your job to go down into darkness?"

I smiled. Why not? After all, I'd been heading that way for a while now.

* Chapter Twelve *

The tunnels of the goblins' underground world weren't actually that dark after the first couple of hundred yards. Certainly, for the first part, they were so dark that Siobhan had to take my hand, guiding me by touch so that I didn't trip and fall. That was just something to keep out the curious, though.

Beyond that first section, the tunnels of the extinct volcano beneath the city had lights set into the walls in a complicated mishmash of electric lights, torches, and simply stones that glowed, apparently set according to whatever the goblins had to hand at the time. For all they'd learned to fear the sun, many of them still craved light. Maybe that was partly because, away in the dark, I was sure I could hear things moving.

"Are you sure we're going the right way?" I asked Siobhan. "It feels like we've been down here a while now."

At least an hour, according to my watch. It was hard to tell if that meant we were close to our destination, or still barely setting out. I'd known about the goblins living beneath the city most of my life, but that didn't mean I'd had an opportunity to wander around their home. Goblins might not fit the stereotypes in most respects, but the rumors of what they did to unwanted guests were still there.

Siobhan nodded. "I know where I'm going. We're just having to take a roundabout route to avoid trouble. Are you still sure you want to do this?"

"Yes, I'm sure." What other answer was there? Niall was down here. I was going to find him. That was all there was.

"I mean, are you strong enough to do this?" In the confined space of the tunnel, it was hard to avoid the slow trickle of her fear. Siobhan had gone along with me because it was her best chance of getting Dougie back, and because she owed me for lying to me, but that didn't mean she had to like this situation.

"I'll have to be strong enough." I tried to sound like I meant it. I was still pretty weak from not having fed. Marie had pricked her finger before I left, allowing me a thin trickle of energy through that break in her body's defenses, but that wasn't much.

I hadn't dared to take much—I couldn't take power from Fergie because he was a werewolf, and Siobhan needed all of her strength to guide me. I wasn't even sure I wanted to try feeding from Siobhan anyway. From what I'd seen, Victoria had already messed her up badly enough with her "explanations" and her threats. Siobhan needed someone in her life she could trust.

Siobhan led me down through twisting tunnels and open caverns, many of which seemed to turn back on themselves, so that we were either descending in a spiral beneath the city, or the presence of so many fey meant that the tunnels didn't bother about little things like the laws of physics. There were times when the tunnels reminded me of the Escher artworks Niall enjoyed, with stairs going in impossible directions.

Geologists said that the volcano beneath the city was dead. That it could never fire again. Yet, the temperature grew warmer as we headed down. Siobhan and I took side tunnels and kept to the shadows where we could, yet I still caught glimpses of goblins and their world as we passed openings and junctions. Here and there were gardens of molds and mosses, glowing softly in the dark. We sneaked by a sort of holding pen where one of the more misshapen goblins I had seen stood guard over things that shuffled behind wooden bars. Was that their food or just something too dangerous to be allowed free? I shuddered in spite of myself as it began to sink in just how different Siobhan's world was from mine. We passed a cave room full of statues, each carved to impossible beauty, just sitting there with moss growing up the bases.

Somewhere down one of the endless tunnels, Siobhan froze. Her pupils glowed silver in the gloom as our eyes met. She whispered, "They've found us."

Softly moving humanoid shapes stepped in front of us and behind. Goblins. I could have pushed out the same kind of not noticing power that I had back at the castle, but for now, it seemed that these goblins were content to stay on the edges of what we could see, never moving closer, simply always there as Siobhan and I kept moving down through their home.

"It looks like we have an honor guard," I told Siobhan, trying to sound more confident than I felt. She looked at me like I was crazy.

Other goblins appeared as we passed branches and openings, not doing anything, just standing there, watching us. They came to stare at us in all shapes and sizes, from slender and beautiful–their skin made almost translucent by the dark–to tusked, and bristling with spiny hair.

"They're funneling us somewhere," I said.

Siobhan nodded, not saying anything. I sensed that she felt too scared to say anything. I put a hand on her shoulder. It didn't help. All we could do was keep going, trying to find the space they were pushing us toward.

We found it soon enough, and when we stepped into it, I couldn't help a gasp of surprise. It was beautiful. Beautiful in a way that I would never have associated with the goblins. The cavern we had stepped into was floored with white and black marble tiles, creating a checkerboard effect. There were mirrors around the walls and chandeliers burning above. A kind of long buffet stood along one wall, by the mirrors. Goblins of all shapes and sizes filled the space. Overall, the effect would have been of a 1920s' ballroom, except for the raised dais at one end, on which sat what could only be described as a throne.

Figures clustered around that throne, young men and women. All good looking, all elegantly dressed. All wore the vacant expressions of addicts, or an enchantress' prey. Where had they gone missing from the world above? *When* had they gone missing? I couldn't help thinking of the missing witches and warlocks Rebecca had told me about. Even if these weren't them, they were just one more proof that Jessica's death had not been sloppy. That Victoria could have made her disappear without me noticing all too easily, if she'd wanted.

Victoria looked perfect, playing the part of royalty. She wore a shimmering dark dress that matched her hair and had probably cost a fortune, along with dark opera gloves that reached above her elbows and just a few pieces of ornate silver jewelry. The goblins around us parted to allow Siobhan and me to proceed forward to the foot of the dais, where I stopped, putting my hand on Siobhan's shoulder to stop her, too.

"So, I'm here." I paused, wanting to make it clear that I understood what was going on here. "Just the way you wanted."

Victoria laughed, and I had to admit that it was a beautiful laugh. "Niall said that you would be clever enough to work it out. To be honest, I had a few doubts after our first meeting."

"At Jessica Hammersmith's house." I nodded. "I thought I could feel your emotions, and you didn't feel like one of us."

"I'm old enough to have learned a thing or two about projecting what I want, and you *did* feel the sense of me in the house."

"Because you wanted me to," I said. I was only too aware of the goblins all around me, yet, for now, at least, it seemed that Victoria wanted to make this a nice, cozy chat. "Because you wanted to play with me. Test me."

"Good," Victoria said, likc a teacher happy with a small child's progress. "You understand, then?"

"Niall tried something similar," I explained. "Only with him, it was an expensive artwork for bait, not a dead young woman. Tell me, did you ever feel anything for Jessica Hammersmith?"

"Of course," Victoria said. "She was beautiful, she had money, and she was deliciously eager to please me. Oh, Jess would do *anything* I wanted, after just a little while."

Clearly, we had very different ideas of what it meant to feel something for someone.

"You addicted her to you like a drug," I said. "You met her…where? At one of those singles' nights you so conveniently pointed me at? You took her and you made it so that she couldn't live without you. Couldn't think without you."

Victoria's expression darkened slightly. "Niall warned me that you would take a dully moral view on this. How distastefully…human. Righteousness is overrated, dear."

I ignored that. There was one thing I couldn't ignore, though. "Are you telling me that Niall knew all about this? All about you?"

She laughed that attractive, bell-like laughter again, but didn't answer my question. "You're still so young. You think that all this is wrong. You'll learn to become an opportunist."

I shook my head. I would never turn into that. "Jessica's life meant so little to you? You just killed her, because it was convenient? Her love meant nothing to you?"

"Why shouldn't we do what we please? Jessica was lovely, but she was human. In a few short decades, she would have been dead anyway. At least this way, she had a chance to serve a useful purpose for something bigger than her human life. I took her at the peak of what she was, like the sweetest peach on the tree. She always told me that she wished things could stay like they were when she was on stage. Now people won't have a chance to remember her any other way."

I wanted to hit Victoria then. "You used her up, and then you made her put a noose around her own neck."

"It was necessary." Victoria said it so evenly. If there was regret there, it was no more than that of a chess player sacrificing a pawn. "She understood that at the end, I made sure that she understood, and her precious sister is well taken care of. How else was I to get you to this point?"

"You could have simply introduced yourself," I suggested. "You know, the way any normal person would have."

Victoria shook her head. "Dear Niall would have warned you away from me. He *tried* to warn me off when he heard I was here, you know. He's been trying to keep the two of us apart. He doesn't think I'll be a good influence."

"Like you were for him?" I asked. "I know all about the handfasting and how he fled you when the year was up. Clumsy, Victoria. He only needed a pair of scissors and a broken heart to free himself from you."

"He still came running when he heard I was here."

Now it was all beginning to make sense. Those secret meetings and Niall's sudden absences. I didn't doubt that on some of them, Niall had been hunting, but how many had been about looking for Victoria? How many had been him trying to warn her against going near me?

"You manipulated all of this," I said.

Victoria's smile was back. She obviously thought it was a compliment.

"You set me a trail of breadcrumbs to follow. You gave me the sensation of an enchantress being there. You led me to the clubs." I thought about Niall pulling me out of the second club I had visited. "You wanted me to lose control."

"I wanted you to see that there is nothing wrong with being what you are." Victoria drummed her fingers on the arm of her chair. "Clearly, Niall has failed to teach you that. The way you feed on people is so delicate, like a bee gathering pollen from a flower. I wanted to see you become who you really were."

I took a guess at the next part. "You had me shot at."

"A little conflict with the coven seemed far more natural than the cozy arrangement you have going at the moment. They are our enemies, Elle."

"Which is why you've taken all these." I nodded at the men and women kneeling around her throne. The coven's missing people, I was sure of it. "You *want* conflict with the coven?"

Victoria stretched languidly. "I want a lot of things, Elle."

I swallowed back some of what I might have said then. "You turned me against Niall. You tried to make me kill him. You framed him for Jessica Hammersmith's murder."

Victoria spread her hands. "Actually, I was fairly confident that you would not kill him. However, I needed him to see that this dream of a life out there with you couldn't work. Not yet."

"Not yet?" I echoed. "Where is Niall?"

"He's safe." Victoria gestured to the goblins around us. "What do you see when you look around this room?"

I looked. I didn't have a good answer. "Goblins?"

"Goblins," Victoria agreed. "A term coined by the coven centuries back to cover all those fey who don't suit their ends. Who don't fit their precious Tolerance Directive. A hundred different varieties of supernatural being, shoved underground and kept here against their will, while humans…weak, foolish humans, get to walk around on the surface as they wish. Free."

"That's what this is about?" I asked. "You…you're talking about coming back to the surface?"

"I'm talking about people being free. About giving the goblins back their place in the world. About taking back what the coven took from us."

"You're mad."

Victoria stared at me levelly. "Is it mad to want to simply be what you are? The coven forced me down here with their hunters. It was either banishment or execution, simply because I was true to my nature."

"Meaning that you killed people," I guessed.

Victoria shrugged. "Yes, and for that they forced me to hide here. Is it mad that I should want that to stop, or are they the mad ones? I've seen you, Elle. I've watched you. You just want to live your life. You want to be free. But to do that, you're putting aside what you are. I can feel the hunger in you that you insist on denying. All because the coven taught you it was wrong. That can never be right. Not for you. Not for any of those here."

"So, you're planning what?" I demanded. "Some kind of mass exodus to the surface? A revolution with goblins as your cannon fodder?"

Victoria smiled. I had struck a nerve.

"That doesn't matter for now," she said. "What matters is that we build our strength. I need you to join us. I went to a lot of trouble to get you to see things as they were. I need to know that you've learned those lessons. I know you have no love for the coven. So, what is that old saying? 'The enemy of my enemy is my friend?'"

"You wish," I replied. I got it then. All of this, Jessica's death, the faked attacks from the coven, everything, had been about recruiting me. She'd separated me from Niall. She'd set me against the coven by making it look like they were attacking me. She'd lured me here.

Oh, she wanted Niall, too. Victoria wanted *both* of us on her side if she could manage it, if not under her thumb. Yet I sensed that in a lot of ways, I mattered more to Victoria. Otherwise, she would have taken Niall a long time ago.

"No, Victoria," I said. "I came here to get Niall and Siobhan's boyfriend, Dougie. That's it. You blew any chance of getting me to help you when you started killing people to get my attention."

"You still don't truly understand what you are, do you?" Victoria asked, standing.

"Niall and Dougie." I looked her in the eye. "Give them back, or the coven gets to hear all about this. They will not take kindly to you using the goblins as some kind of private army. You want to stir up conflict with them? That's one thing, but I don't think you want them hunting you down personally. Hand over Niall and Dougie and let us walk out of here, or you'll have every hunter they can muster coming down here."

"Niall is…indisposed right now, and the goblin boy?" Victoria nodded to someone back in the crowd of goblins. A couple of goblins dragged something forward, depositing it at the foot of the dais. I had never liked Dougie, but even so, seeing his dead eyes staring up was hard. Seeing how it hurt and shocked Siobhan was harder.

"But you promised!" Siobhan yelled, starting forward. "You promised you wouldn't! Dougie!" she cried out in anger and pain.

Victoria caught her, pulling the goblin girl to her in a cruel parody of true comfort. "It's all right, Siobhan. It's all right."

"Let her go!" I demanded, to no avail.

I could feel the waves of emotion Victoria poured into her, pushing the now-unresisting goblin down to her knees beside the throne-like chair, down with all the witches and warlocks.

I reached out with power, trying to help her. I knew I had more potential for power than Niall, so why wouldn't I also be able to eclipse Victoria's strength? I decided to give it a try.

I found out the answer to that almost as soon as I touched the weavings of emotion running through Siobhan, weavings that took her grief and tied her up in it as securely as chains might have.

Victoria was old. Old, and powerful, and well fed. Whereas, I was young, and even if Niall had thought I had the potential for power, I was on the verge of starvation, magically speaking. Every strand of power Victoria had put into Siobhan seemed cable thick and impossible to break.

Worse, they seemed almost sticky, catching my attention, dragging my mind down to tangle in them, too. I barely felt the moment when Victoria's henchmen goblins grabbed me, only looking up when Victoria cupped my jaw gently, forcing me to meet her eyes.

"Teaching is always so hard," she said softly. "Niall ran from me all those years ago, and more recently…well, even with you thinking he was a murderer, he seemed to think it would be betraying you to help me. In fact, he *refused* to help me. His old mentor, his former lover, his wife, can you imagine? So, I've given him some time to think. In time, I'm sure he'll see things my way."

"You—"

Victoria put a finger to my lips and wherever she touched me, it burned—I tried, but could not pull away. "I'm going to give you the same opportunity that I have given Niall. Not because I hate you. Not to punish you. Please don't think that you have made me angry, Elle. I do this only because I have a duty as your new teacher. I want you to learn exactly what you are. Once you understand, I'm sure we'll be friends." Her lips brushed my forehead. "And so much more than that."

I tried to protest but Victoria was so strong that I was unable to even shake my head in that moment. Even though she wasn't even touching me I couldn't say anything. I was too deep in the tangles she had left on Siobhan. In reaching out, I had let her in. I even had trouble drawing a full breath. She was crushing me with her power. Simply crushing me. I fought against her in my mind, to no avail. I was paralyzed.

She looked at the goblins around me with dark intent in her eyes. "Take her to the oubliette. Once she's nice and starving, throw in a human."

Chapter Thirteen

Oubliette. A little place of forgetting. A place to forget about prisoners. The pretty word made a hole in the ground with no way out sound so much nicer than it was. I could have hurt the goblins who held me. I could have killed them, but for Victoria's power at holding me back from struggling as I stood there in the throne room.

"How old are you?" I managed to ask. Even that took too much of an effort. It wasn't that Victoria was controlling me. I was simply crushed by the weight of her power.

She laughed, and as if to prove that the world wasn't fair, it wasn't the laugh of some movie villain. It wasn't equal parts madness and evil. It sounded, if anything, like the laugh of a slightly racy aunt. The one your parents didn't want you ending up like, but probably slightly envied for her freedom to do as she pleased.

"Now, Elle, you know you shouldn't ask a lady her age." She nodded to the goblins. "Take her."

The goblins dragged and shoved me down a dark corridor that smelled of damp earth and mold. One of them opened a locked door with an old-fashioned key before they threw me into the oubliette. Literally threw me. They shoved me down a slippery slope on which I couldn't keep my footing as I fell into darkness.

Though I dropped to my hands and knees and scrabbled for any handhold or foothold I could find, I still slid. The slope fell away into the looming darkness, and then I sailed off an edge, gasping in fear as I touched nothing. I was in free-fall. As I dropped, in that moment, I was hanging in the air. I had a moment to think about the landing that might be waiting for me. Would I break my neck or other body parts? Any broken bone would be bad down here. Were there sharp things at the bottom? Carnivorous beasts? The unknown terrified me as much as the fall itself.

It wasn't some hundred-foot shaft, though. Truthfully, I hadn't expected it would be. Only my fear had tried to tell me that. Instead, I quickly crunched into a hard floor, groaning as I hit it, my breath going out of me. My arms and legs scraped on the stone of the floor, bruising but thankfully not breaking. Around me, it was pitch black.

"I'm going to kill Victoria for this," I said aloud, although that wasn't true. I was going to kill her for everything *else* she'd done. For Jessica Hammersmith's murder, for making me suspect Niall. For the look on Siobhan's face as she saw Dougie lying dead on the floor of that throne room.

"Elle?" Niall's voice came out of the dark, not far from me. "Elle, is that you?"

My heart leapt.

"Niall! It's me," I said. "I came to get you. To save you. But they got me. Victoria got me."

For the longest time, Niall was silent. I sat down in the dark, waiting for him to answer. Wanting to know how badly

I had messed things up, back when I'd accused him of murder.

After a while though, Niall laughed. "You really came all the way down here to save me?"

"Yes. Um… it probably hasn't worked out as well as I would have liked."

"Victoria has used me to trap you." This time, I could feel the regret coming off Niall.

"I know about what Victoria did. All of it, I think." I thought back to what Victoria had said about him going to her to try to warn her off. To him hunting her on the walls of Edinburgh Castle. "Why didn't you just tell me all this?"

Niall didn't answer for a moment. "I never wanted you to know about her. I thought I could deal with this. Drive her away before she got close to you. I thought that if you ever learned about Victoria and the things we had done together, I would lose you. I worried that if you learned about her, you might let her get control of your life, too."

"But if you'd told me, I might have avoided all of this."

"I know, I'm sorry." Niall took a shuddering breath, there in the darkness. "I was barely twenty when I succumbed to her. She was so glamorous. So beautiful. She became my teacher, my lover, everything. I couldn't see beyond her. What Victoria said was the truth, to me. How could it be anything else?"

"What did she teach you?" I asked, even though I already knew the answer. I'd seen the contents of the box Niall kept locked away. I knew what Victoria wanted to teach *me*.

"She taught me to kill," Niall said. "Not every time. Not even most times. But she taught me that it didn't matter if my prey died. She taught me to use people. To get as much from them as possible and then discard them. The first time I killed, I didn't even know that feeding might do so. Victoria was there beside me, urging me on, and it just felt so right."

"Was that why you went to so much trouble to find me?" I asked. "You thought I needed a teacher?"

Niall paused. "Yes. Although I stayed for very different reasons."

Love. We both knew it.

"After I killed the first time, I panicked. I ran. I fled the scene. Young and impressionable, I had let Victoria make me into a killer. Yet, where else could I run but to her? She hid me, for a time, and then imprisoned me, telling me she could only protect me if I gave her what she wanted. If I gave in to what she wanted me to be. What do you think I did, Elle?"

"You married her. I saw the ribbon."

"Handfasted for a year. I did that because it was the least I could get away with. Victoria accepted, because she assumed that with me bound to her for a year, she would soon be able to make me hers in truth."

"She kept you killing," I guessed.

Through the darkness, I couldn't see Niall's expression, but I could feel him. I could feel the pain.

"She kept me killing. She used me to help control people. She told me again and again that they didn't matter. That they were too short-lived to matter. I so nearly believed her. I so nearly became what she was."

"But you didn't," I said. "You cut the ribbon."

"No. I fled her when I could. Ever since, though, I have been frightened. I knew that she would pursue me eventually."

"She's very strong."

"She is ancient."

"How ancient?"

Niall sighed. "You don't want to know. I'm not even sure *I* know, not really. She...she would talk about the past sometimes, so long ago that it seemed ancient, and she would talk about it as though it was yesterday."

"She's that old?" I asked.

"She is so old that the rest of the world doesn't seem real to her," Niall said. "So old that human lives seem like those of mayflies. You wouldn't hesitate to squash a mayfly."

I thought I understood. Victoria wasn't evil, not in her own mind. She was simply so terrifyingly old that no one but her *mattered* anymore. They didn't seem real, the way she was. And because of that, she did things that *were* evil. Undeniably so.

I moved over in the direction Niall's voice had come from. I could feel him there, too. I reached out until I could feel his skin against my hands, then sat down beside him.

"Niall, I'm sorry. So very sorry that I ever doubted you. I thought, I felt..."

"I know, Elle." And that was the thing about what we were. He *would* know. He would always know what I was feeling. How much I loved him. Just as I could feel the love coming from Niall then. It was hard to believe that we could both feel that and still end up so far apart.

"I didn't understand what you were facing," I said. "I didn't understand why you couldn't tell me the truth."

"All that does not matter now," Niall whispered, close to me.

"It matters to me. I should never have suspected you. I accused you of being a killer."

Niall's hand brushed my arm. "I am a killer. I have killed. I told you that. It doesn't go away."

I swallowed. “But you didn’t kill Jessica, you didn’t kidnap Rebecca’s people. I’m sorry. I should have listened to you.”

Niall paused, just briefly. “I made it very easy for you to accuse me. From the start, I could have told you about Victoria. I could have told you how I have been running from her. We could have dealt with this together. Perhaps, we could have battled her together.”

I leaned against him in the dark. I needed that contact just to know that someone else was there. “Why didn’t you tell me? All of this?”

“I did not want the past ruining things here in the present,” Niall said.

“What do you mean?”

“I didn’t want to parade all of my painful mistakes in front of you. I wanted it to fade into the background. Pretend it never happened. Now, it has come full circle again, with Victoria. She has made me her prisoner again.”

“I could have helped you, Niall.”

“Maybe. But it wasn’t just that. I’ll admit, I felt like I owed Victoria something. She was my mentor. She taught me, from the time when I was young. I did not wish to see her killed. I feared her. I loathed what she did to me, yet she brought out my powers and taught me how to use them. I hoped that I could deal with this without her being hurt.”

I could understand that. Even when I had thought Niall was a murderer, I hadn’t been able to bring myself to simply kill him. “I don’t blame you. But I could have helped.”

“I know you would have, but I feared that in the process, she would hurt you. I knew she would find the thought of you irresistible. I thought she might even be jealous.”

“Jealous? Of me?” I found that hard to believe. Victoria was old, powerful, beautiful, dangerous.

"Of you," Niall said. "Because you are everything that she is, and you are more. You are better than her in so many ways. And you hold my heart completely, totally. You have held it since the moment we met, without ever needing to force me to your side."

"I love you, too," I whispered, my lips managing to find his despite the blackness. For long moments, we were caught up in our reunion of kissing and holding each other.

Eventually though, I had to ask him the obvious question. "What's going to happen to us here?"

"Nothing," Niall answered after too long a pause. "That is the point. We have been abandoned here to darkness and regret and shattered dreams."

I didn't bother trying to look around. "A prison cell with no way out."

"Exactly. In the past, long before even I was born, they would throw prisoners into deep cells and leave them in the dark, throwing food down if they remembered. Leaving them to starve if they did not." Niall laughed bitterly. "I fear Victoria was more than a little upset that I would not join her again. Not by her side. Not in her bed."

I caught the drift of that. "She wants your support back in *every* way?"

"Of course she does. It would be proof to her that I was obedient once more. What did she say to *you*?"

"Victoria said something about teaching me what I was." Just the thought of those words scared me. "She said they would throw someone down here with me when I was hungry enough."

"As I said," Niall said, "they would throw down food when they remembered. And once we are starving, we will not be able to stop ourselves."

I understood then. "She wants to make us kill. She means to starve us until we are willing to kill to survive."

"That's right. Just as she did to me. After all, once we have killed, how big a step would it be to doing anything else she wanted? *Anything* else."

Because what else would be left for us? Victoria had already shown me what I would do when I was hungry at the club. I had fed on the bartender through simple instinct. I had no illusions about what might happen if she left me down here long enough. Would killing break me? Would she leave us down here long enough to turn us into something barely human? Would she eventually come for us like some kind of angel to lift us up, so that we would fall at her feet and beg to help her?

"She is relentless." Niall's voice almost broke. "She is old enough to have learned patience, too. She will keep us hungry enough that we will kill and kill."

I thought of all the steps on the road here. All the manipulation. "All of this, just to get us here?"

"Not *us*, Elle. *You.* Victoria could have tried to lure me back at any point in the last hundred years. But she didn't. She left me alone until you came into my life. Only then, once she learned what you are and guessed at your power, did she become relentless in pursuing me again. She used me to get to you. At best, I am a bonus to her. An opportunity to express her…displeasure at being abandoned."

Niall was right. Of course, he was right. I'd thought the same when I'd confronted Victoria. It was too much of a coincidence that Victoria was acting now, so soon after Niall had found me. So soon after my very clear split with the coven.

"But why?" I asked, because that was still the question. "I mean, I know she wants me, but I've felt how powerful she is. Why would she need me? Why would she care?"

"Victoria is powerful," Niall agreed, "but like me, she was never formally trained. She has some knowledge of magic, but only some. Whereas, you have all the knowledge that comes from being the daughter of a coven leader."

"Even so," I insisted, "Victoria is *ancient.* I mean, just to live that long…"

"Our bodies do that automatically," Niall said. "Without the knowledge and training to shape energy, all the power in the world can only go so far. Victoria could take a crowd and make it believe almost anything. Her position with the goblins shows that. She could take one person and make them *do* anything. That part is not in doubt."

"The way she did with Jessica."

"The way she did with Jessica," Niall agreed. "Yet, in a direct confrontation with the coven? Victoria might win, if she caught them off guard. If they were all together. If she broke through their shields."

I couldn't help thinking of the witches and warlocks she had taken. Of the way I had nearly drained Rebecca after we had fought Evert.

Niall went on. "It is more likely though, that she would die. If a witch knows one of us is coming, they can stop us getting close enough to breach their defenses. Even if Victoria won the first battle, she would die, because there are spells that can kill from a distance."

I hadn't thought about that. Did I truly have so much more magic than Victoria?

"She needs you, Elle," Niall went on. "She cannot battle the coven alone."

"Battle the coven? She's really mad enough to go through with that?"

"That's my guess," Niall said. "What else makes all this worth it? How else could her supporters return to the surface? The coven would stop them. The coven would *kill* them."

I could believe that. The coven only tolerated supernatural creatures up to the point where they became a threat. They had attacked me and threatened me, spied on me and betrayed me. And yet…and yet, I still didn't want to be used as a weapon against them. Not by Victoria. Not by anyone.

We couldn't risk it. We couldn't wait around, either, because I was *not* going to sit there and starve until my principles give in. I was *not* going to kill people simply because I am too hungry not to. How long would that take? A day? A week? An hour? If I had fed more over the last few days, we might have had time, but as it was, I knew I wouldn't last long down here. Even Niall wouldn't last forever.

"We have to get out of here," I said.

"How?" Niall demanded. "I have tried. The cell is well designed. I can climb up the slope with an effort, but the door is strong and I can't get the lock undone. As I have discovered trying to break it open, any sudden movement knocks me back down here."

"I have magic," I pointed out. To prove it, I conjured a faint witch-light, letting me see our prison for the first time. I had been trying to conserve my strength, but I was sick of sitting in the dark. The cell wasn't large, no more than a few paces across. It was a smooth-walled stone shaft with a slope high up on one side with a drop-off way above our heads. There was no way of climbing up to it, so Niall must have jumped. I couldn't imagine jumping half that high, as tired as I was.

"Don't waste your energy," Niall said. "You'll need it."

"It's only a witch-light. This is easy, now that I know I can do it."

"I'm glad." Niall did seem genuinely pleased at that small difference in my life. "You have learned so much."

"You helped me discover who I am and what I am capable of." I could hold one of these witch-lights almost without thinking about it now, pulling in tendrils of emotion from around me to power it. Yet, even as I tried it, the light guttered and died. There wasn't any emotion nearby to take in as sustenance. Whoever designed this oubliette, they did a good job of it, with thick natural walls and a location far enough away from anywhere else that I couldn't feel anything of the outside world.

"The isolation is part of the torture," Niall said, obviously feeling the hint of despair that came through to me then.

"Was it here that Victoria held you last time?"

"Not in this oubliette. In another."

"Where?"

"In the Edinburgh Vaults. There is a way through." Niall shuddered against me. "She liked the idea of keeping me hidden, so close to one of the city's attractions."

"The Vaults, really?" I wanted to see Niall's face, but I wasn't sure I had the strength for another witch-light. I was as cut off from emotion to power my magic as I was from light. From hope.

That thought was enough to lend me strength. I pulled emotion from inside me long enough to let me conjure a second light. I wasn't sure how long it would last, though.

I tried to look around for a way out. There were bones in the corners where those before us had crawled off to die. I didn't have enough time to look at them properly though. Instead, I went around the circumference of the oubliette with my light, pouring the little power I had into it, keeping it going with my own energy as I walked my slow circuit.

As I held up my witch-light, I saw that there were names and dates scratched on the walls.

"Niall, look at this. There are names here." I started to read them out, along with the dates beside them. "William Hare. 1828."

"A notorious killer who had to run from the noose," Niall said. "He completely disappeared. I guess we know where. Who else?"

"Robert Gunn. Also 1828." I found myself hoping that he was another killer.

"I don't know him. Perhaps they were down here together."

"There are three names, also together, scratched into the stone: Thomas Marshall, James Ducat and Donald McArthur and the year, 1900."

Niall rustled. "Wait a minute. Let me think. Those names." He sighed heavily. "I remember now. There were three lighthouse keepers by those names. They disappeared from the Flannan Isles. No one ever knew what happened to them. Although why they would end up here, I don't know. Leave this, Elle. We cannot escape."

"You escaped last time."

"No. Victoria threw down sustenance, and I fed. I killed again. I became what she wanted me to be and then she let me out. That was when I escaped her, not before. The best that we can hope for is to do the same."

Niall didn't sound like he believed it would work.

"You don't think we'll be able to get away from her like that, do you?" I asked.

Niall shook his head, barely visible now in the dimming light. "I do not believe she will be so trusting a second time. I escaped because I had a space in which to run. Now, she will have learned. She will keep one of us by her so that the other must obey and return. She will take her time about ensuring our loyalty."

"I don't want to have to kill someone to get out of here," I said. "I know you had to—I don't blame you—but I won't let Victoria do that to me. I won't let her do it to *you* again."

"We cannot stop her," Niall insisted. "You have explored our cell. The door is the only way out. I am strong enough to reach it, but cannot unlock it. You could unlock it, but you do not have the strength to reach it. As for fighting Victoria…she would kill you, Elle. She wants the power you represent on her side, but do not think that she would spare you if you challenged her. She would rather see you dead than rebellious."

I kept making my way along the wall anyway, by rote. Not because I really believed that it would help, but because anything was better than simply sitting there waiting for starvation.

"Are other enchantresses like her?" I asked.

"I do not know," Niall said. "As far as I know, the three of us are the only ones in Scotland. The only ones with our powers, at least. Others of our kind have been hunted down by the coven, and we are rare to begin with. Had you met another like you when you believed you were just a witch?"

I shook my head. "I'd heard about others, but I never got to meet them. I don't know if they're even alive. What are we going to do?"

"Whatever we must."

I would have asked him what that meant, but in that moment, I saw a name scratched into the wall that I knew. *Annette Chambers*. My mother's name. I cried out in anguish and my witch-light guttered out. I didn't have the strength to conjure another. Not now.

"What happened? What did you see on the wall?"

"My mother's name!"

"It can't be."

"It was. I'm telling you, Niall. I saw it. My mother's name, right there. If I could conjure another light…"

"Save your strength," Niall said. "If you say you saw it, I believe you. But what is it doing here? I thought she died in an accident."

"She did. Or that was what I was told, at least."

Why had I said that? Perhaps because I didn't trust anything anymore, not when it came to the coven. Perhaps just because I was so hungry by then that I wasn't thinking clearly. Or perhaps there was more to it than that.

"It could be a trick," Niall said. "Victoria was always one to invent these complex tortures. Maybe she wants to play with your mind."

"I hope you are right," I said, but I wasn't sure what I wanted, right then. I ran my fingers over the spot where my mother's name was, trying to read it by touch.

"Elle, stop looking at a darkened wall and come here."

"I have to find out why my mother's name is carved in the wall of this oubliette! Was she here or was it a trick? And what, if anything, does my mother have to do with Victoria?"

"I would tell you if I knew."

"We can't let Victoria win. We cannot let this be the end of us. Whatever it takes, we have to get out of here."

"Whatever it takes?" he asked.

"I won't kill someone," I said. "I won't do that to someone who isn't willing. We're no better than she is if we do that."

Niall didn't answer immediately.

“What is it, Niall?”

“I love you,” he said. In the darkness, his hands found my face, touching me lightly. “And you will *always* be better than Victoria is. You didn’t trust me before.”

“You didn’t make it easy to trust you.”

“Will you trust me now?” he asked.

“Trust you to do what?”

“Just this.” He kissed me in the dark, his lips finding mine as surely as if he could see them. I could taste his lips on mine, feel the delicious sensation of his lips half open against mine. Niall’s tongue darted into my mouth and I groaned as I kissed him back hungrily. My hands found his hair in the dark, pulling him closer, wanting this. Needing this.

We kissed as though it might be the last time that we had the chance, and for all I knew, it might. I kissed Niall in an apology for everything I had thought about him. I kissed him because he was mine, and not Victoria’s, and my heart was so glad he was.

I kissed him simply because I wanted to. I wanted *him*. It was terrible timing, but I needed Niall with an ache. I let him feel my emotion, as naked as I wished my body were right then. As I wished we both were, because right then I wanted nothing more than the sensation of him next to me. In me.

He responded immediately. When Niall’s hands went to my clothes, I didn’t tell him to stop. He peeled everything I wore from me carefully, but there was nothing slow about it. In less than a minute, I was naked, goose flesh rising both from the touch of cold air and from the thought of what we were soon going to be doing there. That was a good thought, taking this place of suffering and giving it at least one moment of joy.

“Elle. *Elle*.” He said my name like an incantation as his hands explored my skin.

I found the buttons of his shirt by feel, undoing them in the dark as quickly as Niall had peeled my clothes from me. I wanted him then. More than that, I loved him. His hands felt almost burning hot where they touched my skin, and I couldn't get enough of that contact, pressing closer to him as we sought one another by feel and scent and taste.

There in the oubliette, I learned Niall's body a different way, by touch and scent and taste. My eyes already knew how beautiful he was, but now my hands learned his body, too, tracing every contour of his flesh as his fingers moved over me in turn. When they glided into me, I gasped, my back arching as Niall took me expertly to the edge. He withdrew his fingers gently, so tenderly that I moaned at the absence of his touch.

"I want you to remember this," Niall whispered.

He softly pushed me back down onto the warm stone of the oubliette—as warm as the rest of the goblins' tunnels—and the fact that I could feel nothing else in there simply meant that I could feel him perfectly as he pushed himself inside of me. Just the two of us, Niall and me, joined as closely as we had ever been.

I could feel every emotion he had in that moment. There were no barriers between us as I felt every spark of love. Everything he was—and everything I was—unfurled into each other as we moved together there, my hips eagerly moving up to meet his.

I was close, so close, and I could feel that Niall was on the verge as well as he bent over me, his lips finding mine to swallow my cries of pleasure. I felt it then. I felt the first threads of his life energy pouring into me. An enchantress couldn't take from another of her kind, but they could give that energy willingly. They could allow it. Niall was doing exactly that. He was giving and giving and giving.

"Niall—" I was going to beg him not to. I was going to tell him to stop, but now it was too late. My climax washed over me in a wave of pleasure, and that was enough to bring Niall, too. Energy slammed into me from Niall, moving into me as our pleasure bridged the last gap between us, seeming to pour over my entire body at once.

So *much* energy. More than I had, by far. It poured into me, and it didn't stop, moving into me so that I couldn't think, couldn't move. Could barely breathe. I screamed, and I didn't know if it was a scream of pleasure, or a scream of anguish. I knew what Niall was doing and I couldn't see how he would be able to pull back from me in time. No, he couldn't do this. He couldn't.

But he did. Niall breathed energy into me, long after the point where I thought he would stop. Long after the point where it was safe. He breathed energy into me while my back arched in ecstasy, while the pleasure rolling through me was too great to even try to stop it.

When he rolled away from me, I lay there panting in the darkness for long seconds, too weak to do anything else. Yet, I wasn't weak. I could feel the layers of energy burning within me. Rising up from the dark space inside that normally hungered without end, filling up the corners of that silent space until even my skin felt stretched by the power.

"Niall, what on Earth have you done?"

There was no answer in the dark.

"Niall? *Niall!*"

I summoned up a witch-light, knowing I easily had the power to kindle and maintain it. Its flickering light illuminated the inside of the oubliette, showing me our scattered clothes, the rocky walls, and Niall. Niall lay so still in the middle of the floor. So very still. His body was a pale slash on the dark stone floor, as if moonlight emanated from within. But it was a cold light, and dwindling.

"No. *No*."

I moved over to him, trying to remember everything I could about first aid. Trying to work out if any of it would even apply to someone who wasn't human. Niall had given me his energy. All his energy.

Or *almost* all of it, anyway. As I put my face next to his, I could feel his faint breath on my cheek, and he had a pulse, but for how much longer?

"Wake up, Niall."

He wasn't moving. His open eyes stared glassily up at me, and he eerily showed no signs of responding when I called his name. I could barely even feel his presence. Niall had given me so much of his energy that he was comatose, a nearly empty shell.

"No, I never meant for you to do *this*. Niall!"

I knelt beside him, trying to work out if there was anything I could do to restore him. Could I give the energy back to him? Maybe, but then what? We would still be trapped in this hole. We would still be starving. I held Niall's hand in mine, but I knew he had given me the only gift that might get us out of here.

I also knew that he wouldn't have *had* to give me almost all of his energy if I had only been able to bring myself to feed the way I was meant to. If I hadn't restricted myself to secondhand sips of energy from Niall, tiny tastes from his staff. I'd been so afraid of what I might do, so squeamish about the thought of kissing a stranger, that I'd done *this*.

I slowly collected my clothes, trying not to think about it as I dressed, but I knew it was true. I'd starved myself to avoid the act of feeding. I'd held back because I'd thought it was wrong to feel anyone's skin against mine but Niall's, yet did that change what I was? No. It had just left me too weak to protect myself against the likes of Victoria. Perhaps, if I'd fed normally, I might have stopped Victoria from having me thrown down here. If I'd fed, maybe Niall wouldn't have done this.

Maybe he wouldn't have ended up cold and barely breathing on a stone floor in the bottom of an oubliette. I'd been so worried about the meaningless act of kissing a stranger that, for all I knew, I'd lost the man I actually *loved.*

No! I wasn't going to lose him. I wouldn't allow it. Niall had given me his energy for a reason. I wasn't going to waste that chance. I looked back at him once more, knowing that he would probably be safer here in the oubliette than in the middle of a fight. Even so, I couldn't do it. There was no way I could leave my love behind.

I gently dressed Niall and lifted him in my arms, and it seemed so strange to be doing it, carrying the man I loved with such ease. He seemed so light, then. So fragile without any power left in him. That was the hardest part, feeling him like that. So helpless. Niall was normally so strong, so full of life, and now…

Now, I would have to be strong for both of us. I lined up the slope above me, gathered up my power, and leapt toward the tiny circle of light above.

Chapter Fourteen

The door at the top swung open at a word from me. It was as Niall had said before, below. I had the knowledge to get out of there, while he didn't. I had my magic. And now, I had the strength to go with it. Enough strength to leap to the top of the slope. Enough strength to carry Niall easily. I stepped out into the tunnel beyond, still holding Niall, his breathing still steady, but shallow.

I looked down the dimly lit tunnel outside the oubliette. There were eyes there, reflecting the little light that there was. Goblins. There were two of them at the far end, presumably guards.

If some goblins were simply strange looking, or even weirdly beautiful, these were ugly. They fit every stereotype humans had ever had of goblins. Their skin was an ugly greenish-grey in the dark, their eyes small and red. They were hairless, with jaggedly pointed features and ears. Their nails were more like claws, and they hulked in rough rags, their bulk enough to almost fill the end of the corridor. One leaned on a rough club, while the other held a vicious-looking machete.

I recognized one of them. The one with the club had been one of those who had brought poor Dougie's body forward and had dumped it at our feet like old turnips in a sack. He had done it so callously and casually that part of me wanted to simply kill him where he stood. Even so, I gave them both a chance.

"Run," I said, the word carrying easily down the corridor.

They ignored that, of course, stepping forward and lifting their weapons. I lifted a hand in return, whispering more words of magic as they stepped forward to hurt me. I blew out a witch's breath with my spell. One flew backwards to strike the wall with a sickening crunch. The other ran. I let him. I didn't want to put Niall in danger by chasing after him, and it wasn't like I needed to hurt him. I just needed him out of my way.

I made for the throne room. Maybe Victoria wouldn't still be in there. Maybe she would be off in some other part of the tunnels making plans, or simply passing the time until she was ready to start trying to break me to her will. Maybe she was off planning the conquest of the surface, or talking to whatever goblin she'd had shoot at me.

Somehow though, I doubted it. Victoria wouldn't move away from the adoration that came with her throne room. It was too much of a rush for her. It was what she needed.

Well, I needed to end this. And quickly. Niall still seemed stable, like he was just sleeping, but how long would that last? Unable to move, to feed, would he simply fade and die? No, I had to do this now.

"Hang on, Niall," I said. I had half an idea that if I could not bring him back, maybe Victoria could. If she could be persuaded to do that. Niall was so still in my arms. Almost lifeless, but not quite. Inside that shell, I could feel the faintest flicker of life, cut off from the rest of him. I carried him forward with me, back down the path the guards had dragged me along on the way to the oubliette. I knew that my presence would be announced, thanks to the goblin who had run. I didn't care. I *wanted* Victoria there.

Victoria's great hall didn't have as many goblins in it as it had when I arrived—the entertainment of my capture was over, after all—yet there were still plenty, looking around anxiously as one of their number fearfully knelt before the dais, hurriedly explaining to Victoria that I had escaped from the oubliette with Niall.

Victoria sat with an expression of disbelief etched into her features, while around her, her human prisoners and food sources still sat uncomprehending, with Siobhan among them. I glanced over to her and she just stared back blankly, tears still falling silently from her eyes.

"It's true, Victoria," I said, stepping into the hall. "We escaped. And now, I think we need to talk about what you're doing to these goblins."

"You escaped? How did you do it? How?" She stared at me, and then at Niall, obviously understanding. "No, he wouldn't have. He would *never* have given you a gift like that."

I shook my head. "You really don't understand him as well as you think you do, Victoria."

I stepped forward and laid Niall down gently by the dais. I presented him like an offering, but the last thing I would do was offer him to Victoria. This was more like a viewing at a wake. A chance for her to say goodbye.

"You trapped Niall in a hole. You left him to die. You left me to feed on some innocent human. Did you really think that Niall was going to sit back and allow that?"

"Niall, give up his power, for that?" Victoria stared at me in disbelief. "For *you*?"

"For love," I said, "but then, you wouldn't understand that part, would you? Love is just a word to you. Did you tell Jessica Hammersmith that you loved her before you killed her? Have you told the goblins that you love them, and that is why you're leading them to their deaths? Did you tell Niall that you loved him, when you used him and bound him to you, tricked him and made him a killer?"

"I loved him," Victoria insisted. "And he loved me. He cared for me once. He would have again. He would have remembered what we had. Or do you think he loves you?"

I looked at her levelly, wearing Niall's power like a cloak as I stood there with the goblins around me. "I know he does, and so do you."

"You are just a reminder of me. A cheap copy. A curiosity. Your entire family is nothing but an irritation."

My entire family? I remembered the name scratched into the wall of the oubliette.

"Did you know my mother, Victoria?" I asked.

"Know her?" Just the way Victoria said it gave me my answer. "We are not talking about her."

"I think I get to decide that." I was standing in the middle of her throne room, in the exact spot where I had been seized before, but this time I didn't feel helpless. This time, while I had Niall's power thrumming through me, Victoria was the one who should be afraid. "Why is her name carved in the stone wall at the bottom of the oubliette?"

"Is it?" Victoria tried to make it sound casual.

"Did you put her in there?" I demanded.

"You'll never know." Victoria seemed pleased with that, as though hurting me just a little was enough. Had we reached the stage where it was enough to be petty? Victoria had a whole mob of goblins around me, and yet she felt that *this* was the best victory?

"What happened to my mother? Tell me, Victoria. As far as I knew, she had an accident. But the coven never told me the details."

"This is not about your mother."

Victoria was right about that part, at least.

"No, I suppose not," I said. "This is about all the other people you have hurt. Jessica, the goblins, Siobhan, Dougie, who knows how many others. And Niall. Let's not forget everything you did to Niall. You turned him into a killer."

Victoria smiled back at me. "I didn't turn him into anything. I showed him what he was, the way I tried to show you what you are. The way *I* was shown."

I could hear the anger there. I could feel it, washing over me in waves. In that moment, something clicked for me.

"You really believe this, don't you?" I looked around at the goblins she had seduced. Controlled. "You really think this is the only way. Who did this to you, Victoria? Who put you in a hole? Who forced you to kill, and told you that it was the only way you could live?"

"Do *not* try to feel pity for me," Victoria snapped back. "I was powerful when the Romans thought this spot was too worthless to bother conquering. I have seen things, *been* things, that you could never imagine."

"And Niall still chose me over you," I said, simply.

"He was with me long enough," Victoria snapped back. "You think I *forced* him to do everything we did? You know our kind can't control each other's emotions. If he killed, it was because he thought it was right. When we stole from people, it was *him* taking from them as much as me. I'm sure he still does."

"Niall's not a criminal."

"Really? I'd heard rumors of an artwork being stolen that wasn't stolen at all."

"He did that to meet me," I said. "A theft that wasn't a theft, set against a murder. You're going to have to do better than that."

"What about all that wealth of his? The art, the house, the cars? Do you think he gets that by playing fair in his business dealings?"

No, he probably didn't. Niall almost certainly took every advantage his powers allowed him. He hadn't amassed his own goblin army, but that didn't make him perfect. And yet…I'd known that he was dangerous when I first came to his bed. It didn't stop me from loving him. I wasn't sure anything could.

I looked down at Niall's prone form, so still at the foot of the dais. "Look at him, Victoria. Really look. You did this. Do you never stop hurting others? Are you that evil?"

"Probably," Victoria said. I could sense the sadness there, though. "Oh, Niall. He always was beautiful. *And* one for the grand gesture. Even when I was angry with him for leaving me, after the time we spent together, he was too beautiful to kill. Until you came into his life, we mostly left each other alone. So, is it my fault, or yours?"

I swallowed hard. Niall *was* beautiful in that moment, seeming almost to glow, even without power.

"Do you see it," Victoria asked, "the luminescence?"

"Yes."

"That means he is dying," Victoria said. "Niall's body is eating itself up from the inside. He cannot replace the power. He cannot feed. Eventually, a week from now or a month, his body will fail."

"Can you help him?" I asked. This was what I'd been building up to. I could have charged in there ready for battle, but I'd talked first, and this was why. I needed Victoria.

"Of course I can. I *could*, anyway. For a price." It was funny that, so soon after claiming she loved him, Victoria could sit there so calmly, watching Niall starting to fade. That she could talk about prices so casually with his life in the balance.

What else had I expected, though? Victoria might have been like me once, but now… now the damage had been done. Whatever humanity she'd had, it was long gone.

"What price?" It was Niall. I had to ask.

"You stand at my side. You do as I ask. You let me teach you what you need to know." She gestured to the goblins around us. "You help me to give them back what was taken from us."

It sounded such a simple offer, except that I knew what it would entail. Killing and more killing, until I was just like her. Even for Niall, I couldn't do that.

"I have a counter-offer," I said.

Victoria stared at me. "A *counter*-offer? With your love there dying? Are you so cold, Elle?"

Not half as cold as her. The difference was that while Victoria didn't care about anyone, I cared enough to know that Niall would never want me to give in like that. He'd sacrificed himself to make sure that I wouldn't have to.

"Here's my counter-offer," I said. "I gave you a chance before." I looked her in the eye. "I told you to give me Niall and Dougie. Now it's Niall and Siobhan, and the terms have changed. Give me back Niall, release Siobhan, release the witches and warlocks you've taken."

"If I do all that, we'll be friends again?" Victoria asked with obvious sarcasm.

I shook my head. "If you do that, I won't kill you. You'll have twenty-four hours to leave Edinburgh. To leave Scotland. You won't come back."

Victoria laughed again, although this time there was no humor in it. She stood up smoothly and gestured to the lingering figures behind me.

"It *has* been fun talking to you, Elle. Indulging this sense of justice you have. However, you're forgetting one thing. I can still have my goblins put you back in the oubliette. Alone this time."

I smiled. "I thought you might say that. You wanted me for my magic, Victoria. Well, let me show you magic."

The first thing I did was pull the tattered hand fasting ribbon out of my handbag. I held it up for Victoria to see and incinerated it with a word. It was no more than a symbol, but some things mattered.

"You don't have any power over Niall," I said. "He's mine, not yours. He will never be yours again."

Victoria shrieked in fury as the old silk ribbons puffed up into a fireball and rose in the air, only to fall to ashes at her feet.

"No!" she screeched. She gathered her power to retaliate. To crush me the way she had crushed me before. The move with the ribbon had been a mistake, but I had wanted it to be clear. Besides, I had plenty of tricks still up my sleeve.

I threw out an arm and threw magic with it. Not at Victoria, but at the throne behind her. I poured magic into it until it glowed red, and I beckoned, summoning it to me. It shot forwards, striking Victoria in the back. She roared in pain and turned, flinging it out over the crowd, just in time for it to explode in a spray of superheated fragments.

Goblins screamed and scattered. They grabbed their children and each other's hands and backed into the walls in fear. Some of them ran, fleeing the throne room. Others drew weapons, as though wondering whether they should get involved, but not daring to yet.

"No," Victoria yelled in fury, "I'll *kill* you."

Victoria lunged for me, but I was already moving. I'd always known she would deal with the chair. If I'd wanted it to explode where it was, it would have, but I couldn't do that. Not with so many innocent humans around it, not to mention Siobhan and Niall's slumbering form.

No, this was the best I could hope for. Although, when the best I could hope for was making an ancient enchantress so angry that she wanted to tear me limb from limb, maybe I had an odd definition of the phrase.

I dodged Victoria's first rush, kicking out at her knee to give myself space, and then whispered the words to another spell. Victoria threw herself flat as the blast of force ripped through the space where she had been standing, but that just meant she wasn't quite quick enough to dodge as I kicked at her again, catching her in the side this time. She cried out in pain and rolled, coming up to her feet with murderous intent in her eyes.

She swung a slap at me then, and it was fast. Brutally fast, so that I barely ducked underneath it, somehow managing to hook a leg around hers as I drove my weight into her. We caught against the edge of the dais, falling in a tangled mess to the floor. I let go of her and rolled to my feet, knowing that I couldn't stay down with so many people around me. Instead, I swung another kick at her on the floor, one that made Victoria grunt as she blocked it with both arms.

Victoria obviously realized then that a one-on-one fight was what I wanted, because she turned to the goblins around me, looking at them from the floor.

"Grab her. All of you, grab her!"

If I had stayed still, or if the majority of the goblins hadn't still been reeling from the explosion above them, it might have worked. As it was, I danced past the first couple of goblins to come at me, dragging in their fear and anger, transmuting it as I thought of another spell. It was one I hadn't tried before, but with so much emotion coming off the goblins, did it really matter?

I stepped quickly, and it seemed like I left the after-image of me behind as I stepped. I stepped once, twice, half a dozen times in quick succession, illusory copies of me peeling off in quick succession. I pushed away the goblins' attention, letting it slide off me as I had with the crowd at the castle, and suddenly, my goblin assailants were chasing around after the fake versions of me.

"Enough of this," Victoria snapped, pulling herself to her feet, and I could feel her drawing her power into herself as she did it. "Let me show you what power is, girl."

She dragged back power from the goblins. She took it from the chains of emotion that she was using on the prisoners around her. She collected it up until she seemed to pulse with the power of her anger. Then she ran at me, her eyes latched onto me, her hands outstretched like claws.

I dodged, but she followed me, undaunted by the after-images of me that still had the goblins turning in confused circles. The fake versions of me weren't fooling her one bit.

I survived those first few seconds solely because Victoria didn't know how to fight. I guessed that she'd never needed to learn, because she'd always had people around her she could enchant, intimidate, and persuade to fight for her. People she could manipulate and use. She'd always been the one sitting in the background, watching as people fought over her. As people died for her.

Yet, with all that power in her, she was strong. Impossibly strong. Impossibly fast. She had the kind of strength that said just how ancient she was. Just how powerful centuries of feeding had made her.

I barely parried those first blows, struggling to jam her arms and get enough of an angle to survive. Briefly, barely, I saw an opening. Even as I threw a punch though, I realized I had made a mistake. Victoria's blow caught me even as mine struck her, and while mine snapped her head back, hers sent me stumbling.

"I was a fool to think you could be useful to me," she snapped, hitting me again and driving me to my knees. "You are a child, playing at being an enchantress. Too afraid of her own power to ever really use it. You could have killed me with the chair. I wouldn't have hesitated."

She gestured to the humans on the dais, then kicked me onto my back. I thought I felt something break as her foot struck my ribs. I heard it as well as felt it, the snap of the bone coming along with my own small sound of pain.

"You still love them too much. You still think that they're real, these lesser creatures. Their entire lives take place in the blink of an eye. How can that be real?" Victoria leaned down, lifting a hand for a blow that would probably smash my skull. "You still think they matter. You are still far, far too human."

"No, you aren't human enough," I said, as I saw a flash of movement behind her. "And they do matter. They *always* matter."

Siobhan snarled like an animal as she leapt onto Victoria's back, clawing and scratching, biting and twisting. Freed from Victoria's control when the enchantress pulled in her power to fight me, there was nothing stopping her now from unleashing everything she felt over Dougie's death. Victoria screamed and reared up as Siobhan ripped at her throat with claw-sharp fingernails, trying to reach back, trying to stop the sudden blur of teeth, claws, and fury.

It didn't last long. Victoria was simply too strong. A second later, and she threw Siobhan off, standing tall as the goblin girl went tumbling through the air to rest at the base of the dais.

That just meant that Victoria made a better target when I hit her with all the magical force I could muster. The power hit her in the center of the chest, sending her flying back into the middle of the crowd of goblins. A rapidly thinning crowd of goblins. Some had stayed, obviously agreeing with Victoria and her plans to re-take the surface, but others had fled with her influence gone. *Good.* It meant I knew who my enemies were.

Victoria struggled to her feet. She somehow managed to look beautiful even with her dress torn to shreds by the power of the magic I'd thrown at her. Even with bloody scrapes on her arms where the opera gloves had peeled away. She stood, and I could feel her reaching out with her power, reasserting her control over the goblins around her.

"Oh dear, Elle, is that really all you have? All these lives at stake, and that's the best you can do?"

I gritted my teeth against the pain in my ribs as I pulled myself to my feet. I didn't know if I looked half as good as Victoria did as I stood there on the edge of the dais, but I wanted to stand for this.

"No," I said, once I was sure I had Victoria's full attention. "This is."

I reached out and grabbed the emotions of the goblins. I took their fear, their anger, their blood lust, and their hatred. I took the part of them that wanted to see the surface no matter the cost. I took the part of them that wanted to hurt me. I bundled all those feelings up, I poured in the power Niall had given me, and I shaped it with the magic I had.

I threw the whole bundle at the ceiling.

It smashed home on the great chandelier with a sound like two trains colliding. The metal of the chandelier screeched as it twisted, its chains snapping. All that weight hung by a thread for a moment, and then fell in a crash of twisting metal and tinkling, smashing, crashing crystals.

Goblins screamed as they scrambled to get out of the way. Some ran for the walls and pressed themselves into the rock crevices. Some made it. Some didn't.

In the middle of it all, Victoria stared up at the huge lump of metal approaching the spot where she stood. She raised an arm as though that could protect her from the crushing weight. Then she disappeared, dust and metal taking her as the chandelier slammed down.

Above me, the rock the chandelier had been embedded in rumbled as it shifted, a few stones falling down. For now, just for now, everything was still, poised on the edge.

"Siobhan." The goblin girl was down on the floor not far from me. I shook her shoulder hard. "Siobhan."

She looked up at me, apparently barely recognizing me. "Dougie. She killed Dougie."

"I know. I'm so sorry."

"She promised she wouldn't! She gave her word that if I did what she wanted that Dougie would be all right." Her voice sounded so defeated that my heart broke a little for her, even though Dougie had been a rotten boyfriend and a thief, too. That didn't matter, because it was Siobhan who was hurting now.

"Siobhan, we have to get out of here. This whole place feels like it's going to come down, I've got to carry Niall, there are the humans to get out of here, and I don't know the way out. I know it's hard. I know it hurts, but I need you right now."

Siobhan looked round, blinking.

"Get the humans." I pushed her emotions, just slightly, hating myself for doing it. "Get them and lead us out of here,

Siobhan. You're the only one who knows the way. It's a maze up there, and if we take the wrong turn…" I didn't say the rest, but I thought about some of the things I'd seen in the dark on the way down. I didn't want to run into them on the way out.

"Save us, Siobhan," I whispered. "Save us all."

She nodded, and went to round up Victoria's witch and warlock captives. The goblins who weren't dead had run, leaving us behind in the throne room. I knew that Siobhan needed this. She needed to save *someone* today. I didn't count.

I looked up as the rock ceiling groaned. The blast I had put into it had torn out a large section around the chandelier, and now I could hear the rocks as they shifted, grinding and rumbling, slowly working their way to the edge of collapse.

A few more small rocks began to fall. Although these things are relative. They were probably still the size of an average coffee table. They were only small in comparison to the ones around them. The witches Victoria had stripped of their strength and reduced to pets still weren't moving.

I had less of a problem with pushing them to do what I needed them to do, partly because they were still connected with the coven, but mostly because a couple of stalactites chose that moment to dislodge themselves from the ceiling above. They plunged down, embedding themselves in the checkerboard floor like spears.

"Run!" I screamed.

I quickly lifted Niall. He still looked like he was sleeping. It felt so strange for me to be doing something like this with him. I was used to him carrying me upstairs to his bedroom, holding me in his arms. But if I needed to carry him, I would. I would carry him as far as I needed to go to find a way to help him.

"We need to go," I said as we headed toward the exit, and Siobhan nodded, herding Victoria's prisoners out of there as more stones started to fall from the ceiling above. "This whole place is coming down!"

We ran, and as we did, Siobhan let out shrieks and hoots that were utterly inhuman. They sounded like some sort of warning to the other goblins. A warning to keep out of our way. A warning about the rock fall. A warning about what would happen if they tried to stop me now. I wasn't sure.

Siobhan led the way, while I brought up the rear, making sure that we didn't leave anyone behind. I felt as much as saw presences gathering in the dark. Goblins on the edge of what I could feel, their anger mixed in with fear and curiosity. I radiated fear to any I could feel, keeping them back, warning them to keep clear if they wanted to live. I used my power to push them out while we collectively ran for the surface, stumbling and helping each other along, but never stopping.

Never looking back, either. Some part of me told me that if we looked back, the goblins might have fallen on us in a great, baying mob, and even I might not have been able to stop them. Yes, Victoria had controlled some of them, but I was an enchantress, and I knew that some things weren't possible. She couldn't control an entire people just through force of will. They had believed in her. They had believed, and I had just robbed them of their best chance of coming out from the tunnels. That thought was enough to make me run a little faster.

By the time we came up into the air around Arthur's Seat, it was dark. Dark enough that I could barely see the people around me. Dark enough that the stars overhead shone like beacons. I was glad of that, because at least it would keep attention from us, but it also made me wonder about the goblins. Was this what it looked like to them every time they came to the surface? No wonder they wanted it back.

I looked around at all the people Victoria had hurt. They might have been witches and warlocks, but mostly, they were just people. People who looked around blankly in the dark, as though waiting for someone to tell them what to do. Presumably, they had homes and families, places they needed to be. I would have to call Rebecca and get her to help with them. With any luck, them all having the same story would convince her that Niall hadn't been responsible for any deaths in the city.

Niall. He was so still. So drained of energy. Energy that I had used up fighting Victoria. Energy that I had thrown with everything else I had at the ceiling. Energy that I didn't even have to heal myself. Even now, I could feel the edges of hunger creeping back in. I couldn't give him back the gift he'd given me. Not without ending up like him, or worse. So what? Did I simply have to wait for Niall to recover? *Would* he recover without my help? I needed energy to bring Niall back to himself. A lot of energy.

I knew what I had to do to save him. It wouldn't be easy. But it was the only thing I could think of.

Chapter Fifteen

Practically glowing with power, I stepped out of the club. I stared up at the night sky, and for once, I didn't feel the rush of a hundred people's emotions fading as I left. This power wasn't that kind. It was sustenance, not just a taste. I headed back toward the car that would take me to Niall's home. Niall's driver, David, was waiting for me as I got in.

"Did everything go okay, Miss Chambers?"

I thought of all of the lips that had touched mine that night. I thought of all of the hands that had brushed over my skin. I thought of all of the people I had moved so close to, taking a brush of energy here, a brush of energy there. I'd stood in the middle of the same club Victoria had tried to get me to lose control in, and I'd called them to me.

"Everything went fine, David."

I hadn't gone very far with any of them. Never much more than a simple kiss, yet even so, everything about my upbringing told me that I should feel awful waves of guilt, not the faint euphoria that was actually there when I looked down into myself. I could tell myself that this was wrong as much as I liked, but Victoria had been right about one thing: this was what I was. I couldn't deny the hunger, any more than I could simply leave Niall as he was.

I could control how I fed that hunger though. There was no blood. No manipulation. I didn't have to kill people. I didn't have to turn them into the kind of empty, easily cowed shells Victoria left. I certainly hadn't been about to feed on the people I had only just saved from her. That would have been, not just hypocritical, but simply evil. They hadn't had enough energy left for it to be safe. And truthfully, if I had tried to feed on them and they let me, I would have had no way of knowing if they were really doing it freely, or just because Victoria had broken them so much that they thought it was normal.

"And you're okay, Miss Chambers?" the driver asked.

I nodded. "I'm okay, David."

At least in the club, I knew that the people around me had wanted the little I gave them, even if they hadn't known about what I took from them in return. I'd even sent a faint pulse of happiness through the place, lightening the mood a little, turning it into what would probably be a great night for everyone there. It had seemed more than fair.

David drove me back to Niall's place at a sedate speed. We had quite a welcoming committee. Marie and Kelly were there, obviously, because where else would they be? They obviously cared enough about Niall as an employer to want to make sure he was safe. Both they and David had offered to let me take energy from them for this. I'd only refused because I knew Niall needed more than they could provide. I'd already taken too much from all three of them in the past few weeks.

Fergie was there. Partly, he was there to make sure no one attacked Niall's house or staff while I was gone. Mostly though, he was there because Marie was. I noted that they were holding hands. That was good. She'd seen him nearly transforming, seen the worst of him, and it hadn't ruined things for them. She'd just accepted it. Things might have been a lot easier for Niall and me in the last few days if I'd been able to do the same.

Finally, Siobhan was there. Well, she didn't have anywhere else to go, and I couldn't just leave her. I doubted that things would be safe for her back Underneath. I'd felt the resentment that had followed us out of the goblins' home. The anger. I didn't want that coming down on her just because she'd helped me.

"Is there any change?" I asked them.

Marie shook her head. "Everything's the same as when you left."

I nodded. I hadn't expected anything else. I went upstairs to Niall's bedroom. He looked almost angelic, laid out on the bed like some pale, golden-haired sleeper. He looked so much more innocent like that than he did while awake. I paused, thinking back to what I'd just done. Sometimes, innocence wasn't what the world needed.

It was time.

I leaned over him, bringing my lips to his. I kissed Niall softly as he slept, and as I kissed him, I pushed my newly taken power into him. He'd done it for me, when I was just learning how to feed, and then again in Victoria's oubliette. Now, I was the one who shared my power with him. I gave him energy the way someone might breathe oxygen into a drowning man. Second by second, I breathed power into him, letting it drain out of me like water from a dam. I kept going until I didn't have anything left to give. I stopped just short of draining myself into unconsciousness.

Niall gasped underneath me, his eyes flickering open. I hugged him hard enough that he actually groaned in pain and I jumped back.

"You're alive. Niall, you're alive!"

He grimaced. "I really hope that way of putting it, doesn't mean you've just done something unfortunate involving a lightning rod and a very big lever, Elle."

I smiled at that. "This one was more Sleeping Beauty than Frankenstein."

Niall's hand went to his lips. He half closed his eyes. "You fed me. Yet to do that, you must have..."

"I'd do a lot more than that to save you." I couldn't help staring at him.

"Everything, in its own time." Niall took my hand, kissing the inside of my wrist right where the pulse was thrumming. "Thank you, Elle. I can guess how hard it was to do."

I swallowed. I knew there were things I needed to say. That we both needed to say. "I'm going to stop running from what I am."

"That's good."

This wasn't going to be all one way though. "But you need to tell me things, Niall."

Niall smiled. "I'll try. I suspect we both will. Speaking of telling things, what did I miss?"

"Victoria is dead."

I caught the small flash of pain there as I said it. I could understand that. The past didn't suddenly go away simply because of the present.

"You're sure?" Niall asked.

I shrugged. "I didn't see the body, but I dropped half a cavern ceiling on her, Niall. Stalactites. I don't care how old she was, or how powerful she was, she isn't coming back from that. No one could."

"You're probably right," Niall said.

"Probably?"

"Probably."

"And I burned the hand fasting ribbon in front of her. I wanted her to be clear about that part before I killed her."

He leant up to kiss me. "Does this mean I'm all yours now?"

I sighed. "Did I mention that you're a lot less trouble when you're asleep?"

Niall just kissed my hand again. "What else?"

"Well, we've given some of Victoria's coven victims to Rebecca to help. That has at least shown her that we're trying to save people. It might get her off our backs for a while. Oh, and we've acquired a goblin."

"That little thief of yours?" Niall asked, looking suddenly concerned. "Elle, I know most of my more valuable pieces are no longer in the house, but even so…"

"Relax," I told him. "Siobhan will be coming home to my place, not your home and not my office. She can have the sofa. Maybe she can help out around my office during work hours. She needs to do something with Dougie dead, or it will eat her up."

"The goblin boy died?"

I nodded slowly. "Victoria had him killed, to punish Siobhan for associating with me…with us."

"And you need to help her now because you feel guilty." Niall obviously caught my expression. Or just felt what I was feeling. It wasn't exactly easy to keep anything from him. "I'm not saying that it is wrong to help her, Elle. I'm saying that you should not feel guilty. Victoria did what she chose to do. You could not have changed that, even if you had known."

I knew it was true, but even so, there was a part of me that wished I had killed her when I first met her. "I need to help Siobhan. She has no one else and she helped me. If it weren't for her, I probably wouldn't have found you down there."

Niall sat up, stretching back against the bedstead. “I love that about you. That, even for goblins, you can manage such moments of compassion.”

I found myself thinking of Victoria, and the way she’d thought about people and manipulated them.

“Does it get harder, as you get older?” I asked him. “Does it get harder, when they don’t ever seem to live as long as you do? Does it ever feel like no one else really matters?”

Niall looked at me for several seconds. “You’re asking me if you’ll ever wake up one day and find that you have turned into Victoria?”

I nodded. I had a lot of fears for the future. The coven. What Niall and I would do. What the goblins might do once they recovered from the damage to their home. That fear, though, was worse than all of them.

He shrugged eloquently. “I do not know what to tell you. It could happen. It could happen to me. I can’t tell you for sure what the future will hold. I will tell you that I would bet against the sun coming up before I bet on you becoming her. You’re two different people. I can’t see you on a throne making people, or goblins, come to you on bended knee.”

“But you can’t know.”

“I know,” Niall insisted. “It wasn’t age that made Victoria like that, though I suppose it might have helped. It was who she was. She has never been any different.”

“You’re sure?” I asked, because that was one thing I couldn’t face. Niall had only known her for a hundred years or so. He couldn’t truly say what Victoria had been like when she was young.

I didn’t want to end up like her. I didn’t want to think, a hundred years from now, that people didn’t matter. That they would just be my slaves or my meals. I thought about what she had said, about being powerful when Rome first came to

Britain. Had something happened back then to make her the way she was? It was impossible to know.

"You won't be like her," Niall assured me. "I won't *let* you. Just as I hope that you won't allow me to become that, either. I felt betrayed up on the walls of the castle, but looking back…looking back, there is a part of me that is glad you were prepared to do that."

"I'm just sorry I got things so wrong," I said.

"It's done now. It's over. Victoria is gone."

I nodded, although I think we both knew that things wouldn't be that simple. Victoria had used her powers to improve her place with the goblins, but did I really believe that it was just her powers that had them on her side? No. I didn't know how many of the goblins it was, or how strongly they felt it, but at least some of them wanted to get back into the daylight world. That wasn't going to stop simply because I had stopped Victoria.

Worse, the coven probably knew all about it by now. The same people who would have told Rebecca that I wasn't a threat would also have told her all about the goblin menace beneath the city. That could make things pretty tense with the coven. In fact, we'd probably be lucky if they didn't suggest sending strike teams down into the tunnels. I'd have to talk to Rebecca about that.

For now though, it was over, and there were more mundane things to think about.

"I don't know about you," I said to Niall, "but I'm famished. For real food, I mean. Do you want to go downstairs to the kitchen and maybe let everyone know that you're all right?"

"I'd rather stay here with you," Niall suggested. "Let's not forget that the original version of *Sleeping Beauty* involved rather more than a kiss. I'm feeling a little shortchanged here."

A kiss was all he got though. "How about if we head down, grab some food, and then come back upstairs with it?" I suggested. "That way, we wouldn't have to leave the room for a while."

"Well, when you put it like that…"

So, Niall dressed and we headed downstairs. The others were already in the kitchen, where it seemed Kelly had killed time by cooking enough food for about twenty people. They were all happy to see Niall, although Fergie frowned slightly when Marie hugged him. I sensed the slight flare of his jealousy, but put it down as pretty natural for the situation. When we reached Siobhan, Niall put a hand on her shoulder.

"I'm told that you helped Elle to save me. Thank you for that. I owe you a debt."

"T-thank you." Siobhan shook his hand nervously, obviously shocked that someone like Niall would say something like that to her and promised that she wouldn't steal anything while she was there without even being asked. Niall seemed satisfied with that.

She still seemed pretty nervous, though.

"What is it, Siobhan?" I asked.

She shook her head. "It's just…I don't know. What am I going to do now?"

"You're going to stay up here with us," I said. We settled in around the kitchen table, starting to eat. Niall seemed so relaxed there, so natural. Marie and Fergie sat next to one another, close enough to touch. With Marie that close, Fergie didn't even think about complaining that we were about to acquire a thief for the business. Or maybe, he had a softer side in there somewhere, too.

It would have been so simple to just sit there, eat, and talk. To just pretend that things were done with, but there were still a few things that needed to be settled.

"Have you decided what we're going to tell the insurers in the morning?" Fergie asked.

Niall raised an eyebrow at that. I knew what he meant. That we could hardly put the real circumstances of Jessica Hammersmith's death in an insurance report.

"We have to put something," I said. "Jessica has a little sister. One she was helping to support."

"I could see that she gets money," Niall offered, and it was a generous offer. Just to reach out and offer enough money to help bring up a girl he'd never met. "It would be right, my paying for something that has come out of my past to hurt her family."

I put a hand on his arm. "And that's one reason why I don't want you doing it." It wasn't Niall's fault, it was Victoria's. "Fergie, tomorrow, tell the police and the insurers that Victoria plied Jessica with a cocktail of drugs before putting the noose around her neck. That she murdered her, and now she seems to have made a run for it. It's the closest thing to the truth we can give Jessica's sister."

"Is a murdered sister better than one who killed herself?" Niall asked.

I shrugged. "I don't know, but the truth will be better than a lie. It should give her the insurance money, at least. It will tell Jessica's sister that Jessica didn't abandon her like that. It will also mean that the police are looking for Victoria."

"You said you were certain that she was dead," Niall pointed out.

"And you *weren't* certain. Consider this a part of learning to trust you. I figure that the police will let us know if there is ever any sign of her surfacing. Plus, they'll do a little digging into Victoria's affairs for us."

"Is that a good thing?" Marie asked. "I mean, if she's like you…" She stopped. "Sorry, I didn't mean…"

"It's all right, Marie," I said. "And yes, it's a good thing. She had my mother's name on the wall of her oubliette, so I want to know all about what she has been doing for the last few years."

"A good move," Niall said from beside me, reaching out to take my hand.

"And if anyone knows all about manipulating people, it's you," I said, but for once, I said it with a smile. It was a part of Niall I could learn to accept. A part I would have to accept, if it wasn't going to tear us apart.

Niall nodded an acknowledgement of that. "But do not assume that Victoria had your mother as her prisoner, or even that she was there. Victoria lied as naturally as breathing. She always had a knack for the things that would hurt people the most."

"If she *didn't* have my mother, then I want to know that, too," I said. "I just want to know what's going on, Niall."

Niall nodded. "And we will find out. All of us."

The others nodded too. Fergie took a bite of food. "It occurs to me that while I'm pointing the police at Victoria, I could mention the coven's assassination attempts to them, too."

"That wasn't the coven," I pointed out.

Niall seemed to be in a mood to agree with Fergie for once. "The four at the castle were."

I shook my head. "And they were hardly trained battle witches. I think they were probably just the first people Rebecca could find. Victoria wanted to set us against one another. We shouldn't let her succeed, and we *don't* want this out in the open."

"Which is why I wouldn't bring up anything officially," Fergie said. "Certainly nothing about magic. I'd just... happen to mention a few things to a friendly detective or two."

At which point, the Lothian and Borders police force would start paying more attention to the coven. Forcing it to keep a lower profile. Just generally making life more difficult for it. Even so…

"I don't know," I said.

Niall smiled across at me. "I do. Excellent thinking, Mr. Black. And now, I think we have spent far too much time talking about business, when we should be enjoying our meal."

He had a point. We could have discussed the potential threat from the coven forever, along with the risks of the goblins coming after us, the possibilities of the future…but there came a point where it was enough just to enjoy dinner among ourselves. The immediate threat was done with, Niall and I were okay again, and the coven wouldn't come after us until at least tomorrow. It was enough.

So, we sat there and ate, and talked, and occasionally laughed. We talked until it was obvious that Niall was getting impatient to take me back to bed, and by that point, frankly, I was getting a little impatient for it, too. Thankfully, it seemed that an enchanter and an enchantress wanting to go to bed together was an acceptable excuse for wanting to run off from the dinner table. At least from this one. We said our goodbyes and started to head upstairs.

Siobhan caught up to us just as we reached the stairs. She'd been quieter than the others through dinner, but now she looked at me urgently.

"Elle, can I talk to you for a minute?" She looked over to Niall. "Privately?"

Another time, I might have asked her if it could wait, but after everything she'd been through, I guessed that she deserved better than a brushoff. Besides, the last time I'd been too busy to listen to her, things hadn't exactly turned out well.

"I'll wait for you upstairs," Niall said gently. "Don't be too long."

"I won't. What is it, Siobhan?" I put a comforting arm around her shoulders as Niall headed upstairs. "Is it Dougie? I know that you must miss him."

Siobhan nodded and her face fell. "I do."

"I'm truly sorry for your loss. It will get better." I squeezed her tighter. "I know it doesn't feel like it will, but it will. I promise."

I thought back to how I'd felt after my mother died, and I knew that I would do everything I needed to do to make sure that Siobhan was happy. She was stuck here with us above ground. She'd lost the goblin she loved. Despite that, I would find a way to make it work. I owed her that, but it was more than that. I'd thought of Siobhan as my informant for a long time, but the truth was…she was my friend.

Siobhan shook her head. "It's not that. I mean…it *is* that. I know you didn't like Dougie. I get that. There were times when…when I didn't like him much either."

"It's complicated, isn't it?" I said. "Loving someone. You don't get to choose."

Siobhan nodded. "But at least you have Niall. I had Dougie, and…and I *knew* what he was like, but I loved him. Now…now that he's gone forever, I'm not sure what to do."

"About what?"

"Everything. Where to live, how to live…" Her voice trailed off as she started to cry.

How had my life changed to the point where I could possibly consider standing there comforting a crying goblin girl normal? I didn't have an answer to that, so I just held Siobhan. She was so thin and her hands were so cold. I brushed that white-blonde hair from her eyes.

"I'm sorry you lost him. Cry if you need to, Siobhan," I said. "It's okay if you need to grieve. I will try to be there for you. We all will. It will be okay, I promise. Whatever it is, whatever's going on, we'll find a way to make it okay."

"It's not okay, and it's not going to *be* okay," Siobhan said, looking up at me as I held onto her. Goblin features looked odd enough without adding the puffiness from crying to them. "It's…"

"What is it, Siobhan? Whatever it is, you can tell me."

"It's…" Siobhan took a deep breath. "I think I'm pregnant."

The End

***

Elle and Niall will return in
Witch Way Out
(The Witch Detectives No. 3)

About the Authors

Eve Paludan is a mystery and romance writer who lives on the west side of Los Angeles, California. She also edits for bestselling authors.

Stuart Sharp is a writer, ghostwriter and historian based in East Yorkshire. Having dabbled in urban fantasy, he currently writes comic fantasy.

Made in the USA
Coppell, TX
18 July 2021